D1098772

C017066416

A MESSAGE FROM CHICKEN HOUSE

Lucy's amazing landscapes are almost like characters in their own right. In this story, the marsh, its mysteries and its dangers are totally spellbinding. Combine that atmosphere with an intense sense of family, sisterhood, inheritance and even the power of reading and you have a combination that unlocks, for me, the same magic that you'll find in the greatest classic novels. But that's not all: Lucy even finds time for some lovely laughter and one of my favourite ever animal heroes too! Enjoy!

BARRY CUNNINGHAM
Publisher
Chicken House

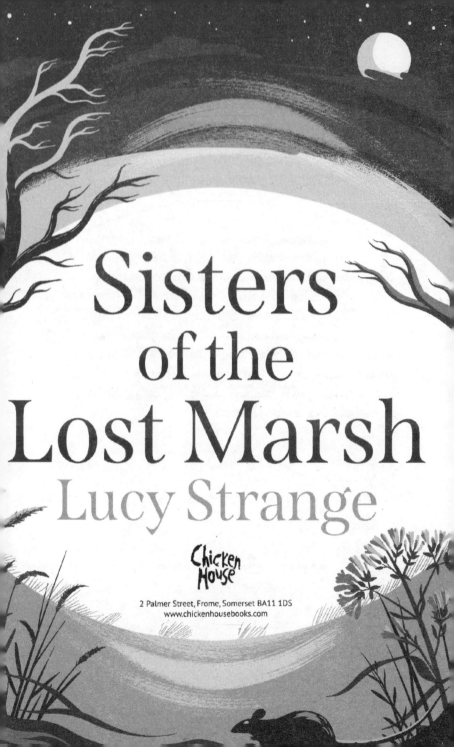

Sisters
of the
Lost Marsh
Lucy Strange

Chicken House

2 Palmer Street, Frome, Somerset BA11 1DS
www.chickenhousebooks.com

Text © Lucy Strange 2021

First published in Great Britain in 2021
Chicken House
2 Palmer Street
Frome, Somerset BA11 1DS
United Kingdom
www.chickenhousebooks.com

Chicken House/Scholastic Ireland, 89E Lagan Road, Dublin Industrial Estate,
Glasnevin, Dublin D11 HP5F, Republic of Ireland

Lucy Strange has asserted her right under the Copyright, Designs and
Patents Act 1988 to be identified as the author of this work.

Cover and interior design by Helen Crawford-White
Typeset by Dorchester Typesetting Group Ltd
Printed and bound in Great Britain by CPI Group (UK) Ltd, Croydon CR0 4YY

FSC
www.fsc.org
MIX
Paper from
responsible sources
FSC® C020471

1 3 5 7 9 10 8 6 4 2

British Library Cataloguing in Publication data available.

PB ISBN 978-1-913322-37-3
eISBN 978-1-913696-36-8

For my brothers, Will and Pete

Be sure the first girl marries well,
The second in the home to dwell.
A third maid can do little harm
If set to work upon the farm.
Four and five must both be wed,
Or six will bury you stone dead.

'The Curse of Six Daughters'
Traditional rhyme from
Hollow-in-the-Marsh

PART ONE

Midwinter

In winter, the light lies
cold and flat on the water.
The rushes of the marsh are
furred with frost, and silver
gilds each thistle . . .

May Fernsby, 'The Forgotten Village',
Tales of the Marshes

I

I am looking into the eyes of an enormous white horse called Flint. They are glossy brown, like puddles after fresh-fallen rain, with long black eyelashes. I hate him – this big, stupid creature we've been given in exchange for my eldest sister.

Silas Kirby brought him over to our farm the morning after the betrothal.

'That's a good ploughing horse for you, Nate Fernsby,' he said.

'That's a good *anything* horse,' Dadder replied, squinting into the cold sunshine and stumbling down the steps. He looked the horse up and down and nodded, impressed. Then he said, 'Check him over for me, Willa.'

Dadder doesn't know the first thing about animals.

It isn't even his farm, really – it's Grammy's. Everything we know about farming, we've learnt from her. Dadder likes to dish out orders, and he swans about at market like a gentleman farmer, but he doesn't know one end of a beast from the other.

Flint stood still in the frosty muck of our yard while I inspected him, running my hands over his big shoulders and strong back. He danced about a bit, making it tricky for me to check his hooves. He jerked away when I tried to see his teeth. 'You're a lively fellow, aren't you?' I muttered. And Flint tossed his head proudly.

At last I was done. I nodded at Dadder, and his eyes widened with a sort of baffled glee that someone should barter such a magnificent animal for one of his wretched daughters. Like gold for a sack of dung.

'Walk him up and down a bit, Willa,' Dadder said, and then he watched as Flint clopped steadily over the cobbles and back again.

'Will you be wanting to give Grace an inspection too, Mister Kirby?' I said, looking him right in the eye. Dadder glared at me, but Silas laughed, and my little sisters were delighted.

'*Grace!*' Dolly shouted at once, running to the door, with Deedee close behind. 'Mister Kirby needs to check your *feet*!'

Darcy, the youngest of the triplets, rolled her eyes at them.

Grace met Dolly and Deedee on the step; she was coming out to take kitchen scraps to the hens.

'Here she is!' Dadder was still half-drunk, after striking the betrothal the night before, so his smile was like the grin of a hollowed-out turnip. 'My beautiful Grace! Soon to be *your* beautiful Grace, eh, Silas?'

Silas Kirby smiled and bowed to Grace.

She walked right past him to the henhouse, where the chickens were all aflap for the scraps. We waited for her to come back, and when she did, she didn't go to Silas; she went to the horse instead.

So this is what I am worth, Grace seemed to be thinking, and perhaps Flint was thinking the same thing. He turned his head towards her and the two of them looked at each other. Then Flint pushed his nose into Grace's open palm. She stroked him and patted his neck, smiling with her eyes in that gentle, dreamy way of hers. Then she stopped. Her fingertips had found something I'd missed: a thick, shining scar hidden by the horse's mane.

We all looked at Silas.

'That were from breakin' him in,' he grunted. 'Bit jumpy as a colt – too cocky by half – but he's more settled now. He'll be a good boy if you're firm with him. Born two summers ago to my grey mare Silver – best broodmare on the marshes . . .'

But Grace wasn't listening. She had closed her eyes and was resting her forehead against Flint's.

Dadder pushed past his eldest daughter. He squinted at the scar on Flint's neck. 'Ar,' he said. 'Some beasts need remindin' who's in charge. Won't have done him no harm.'

'Excuse me,' Grace said quietly, and I don't know if she was talking to us or to the horse. She stroked his nose again, then she turned to go back inside. 'I have to tend to the fire.'

Silas smiled slowly, and his gaze followed Grace as she walked up the steps to the kitchen door. Then he and Dadder shook hands.

We argued that night, Dadder and me – even worse than usual.

'You *sold* our Grace!' I screamed at him as he shoved me out of the kitchen door. 'Daughter-pedlar!' I bellowed from the middle of the stinking puddle I landed in. 'You PIG!'

It was a terrible cold night, so I had to shelter in the henhouse. My thoughts raged around and around – louder than the winter wind, and wilder too. The anger kept me warm though, at least for a while.

It was very late and the shivering was bone-deep by the time the triplets managed to get to the kitchen door to let me in. Dolly and Deedee put their fingers to their lips, giggling 'Sshh!' and Darcy nodded towards the chair by the fireplace, where Dadder was snoring – head back, mouth open, a bottle of grog lying empty on the floor by his feet. I felt all the anger come barrelling back again: while I had been huddling in the foul straw of the henhouse, Dadder had been toasting his toes by the fire, and toasting his seedy little deal too, I'm sure.

My little sisters scampered up the stairs and into our room. They dived into their beds, Dolly and Deedee pulling the blankets up high so only their pigtails could still be seen on the pillows. 'Thank you,' I mouthed to Darcy, and she gave me a serious salute before disappearing beneath her own blanket. I sat down on my bed, cold and aching and tired. My anger had squashed everything else out of me – I felt flattened by it all. I peeled off my damp clothes, put on my nightgown and blew out the candle.

Six beds crammed into one cold room, like cattle stalls.

Six sisters lying there in the dark, the midwinter moon watching us all through the frosted window.

The triplets wriggled for a bit and one of them coughed, but eventually their breathing softened into sleep.

'Grace?' I whispered. 'You awake?' I wanted to know what had happened after I'd been chucked outside; I wanted to know if my big sister was all right.

'Go to sleep, Willa,' muttered a lump in the bed next to me. 'You've caused enough trouble today.'

'Go to sleep yourself, Freya,' I hissed. I tried again,

louder this time: 'Grace?'

A pillow thumped down hard on my face: 'Go to *sleep!*' Freya growled. Then, 'Oof!' as I thumped her right back. 'I hope you're next,' she grumbled. 'I hope Dadder sells you to Old Grubb the pig farmer and we get a nice fat pig in return – at least then we'd have bacon for breakfast.'

'*You'll* be next, Freya, not me,' I whispered. 'You're only a year younger than Grace, and I'm just twelve. And anyway, we have to stay at home to look after the house and the farm, don't we. It'll be Dolly and Deedee that Dadder marries off next – like the curse says. They won't be old enough for another nine years though . . .'

'Oh, shut up and *go to sleep!*' Freya groaned, heaving her pillow over her head for another mighty thump.

Then the door opened, and I froze. *Dadder?*

A candle appeared, and caught me in its light: kneeling up on my bed, pillow held aloft and ready for battle. An arm followed the candle into the room, and then a face, peering at me through crinkled-up old eyes.

Not Dadder. Grammy.

'Is that you, Willa?' she whispered. 'Found your way back indoors, I see. You all right?'

'I'm all right, Grammy. Just . . . trying to get comfy.' I made a show of plumping the pillow I was holding, put it back on the bed and pulled up the scratchy blanket (it was my turn for the horsehair one tonight). 'Goodnight, Grammy.'

'Goodnight, Willa.' The candlelight shifted as our grandmother looked at the lump in the bed next to me, pretending to be asleep with a pillow clamped over its head. 'And goodnight, Freya,' she whispered. 'Sleep tight.'

After the door closed again, I waited for Freya to doze off, then I tiptoed over to Grace's bed and gently touched her shoulder. She gasped, moving her head as if she were drowning in her dream. I stroked her hair, bronze in the moonlight. 'Don't worry, Grace,' I whispered. 'We're here. We'll look after you.' I stroked her until she quietened. I sang the old lullaby she'd always sung to us when we couldn't sleep – it was one of Mammer's songs:

'*A damsel slept beside a brook, a-dreamin' and a-dreamin'.*
The sky was black, the stars were bright, the waxen moon was gleamin'.
The rain fell soft, the sun arose, the winter was a-creepin'.
But still the damsel dreamt and dreamt, a-cursed to e'er be sleepin'...'

Then I kissed Grace's hair and crept back to my own cold little bed.

As I lay there under the awful scratchy blanket, I thought about the deal that had been struck in our farmyard that morning – a horse for a girl. I thought about Silas Kirby: a man twice Grace's age, whose whip-fearing dogs carried their tails between their legs . . . And Grace had been so calm about it all, so dignified.

She was being obedient, I thought. *Softly spoken, sweet-natured, Grace: afraid to curdle Dadder's good cheer, wearing a mask to hide her fear.*

But now I think the mask hid more than just fear. I think Grace was already trying to think of a way out: a way of escaping from Silas Kirby and Dadder and Hollow-in-the-Marsh for ever.

2

Dadder rose late the next day.

I had stabled Flint with our old farm horse, Jet, and while I was forking their steaming muck from the straw, Dadder just stood there, leaning on the stable door, gawping at the splendour of his new horse. I could tell what he was thinking: *I'll be quite the gentleman riding Flint – quite the gentleman!* The gentleman he had always dreamt of being. Then he set off to meet Silas at the alehouse, wearing the same reeking clothes he had fallen asleep in last night.

I stood at the gate with the triplets, watching as his shape grew smaller against the glare of morning sun. The moment he had vanished into brightness, they looked at each other, then looked at me – three wicked smiles on three shining faces. Without saying a word, we all bolted across the yard, leapt the puddles and the steps and slammed through the door into the kitchen.

'He's *gone*!' Deedee yelled, and Dolly ran to the foot of the stairs: '*Grammy!* Dadder's gone to the alehouse!'

'Well, come up, then!'

And they thundered up the stairs.

'Boots!' called out Freya, without even turning around. She was kneeling by the fire, cutting carrots into the heavy-bottomed pan. One by one, six muddy boots tumbled back down the stairs. I picked them up and stood them by the door. Then I wiped up all the mud while Freya poured water into the pan, hung it from the iron pot hook and swung it over the glowing fire. I put a lump of turf on to keep the heat smouldering.

'Middlin' good work, Willa,' Freya muttered (which is about as close as she ever gets to saying anything nice to me or the little ones).

I grinned. 'You'd miss me if I was sold to Old Grubb the pig farmer.'

'P'raps,' she admitted. 'But only a bit.' And she shoved me towards the stairs. 'C'mon, let's go up.'

'Where's Grace?'

'In with Grammy already, I think . . .'

When we opened the door to Grammy's room, Grace was there – sitting on the broad windowsill, with her arms wrapped around her knees. Her face was turned away from us, gazing out across the morning-bright marshes. I wondered if she had been talking to Grammy about the betrothal.

The triplets had no idea what their biggest sister was facing; they were all bright-eyed, sitting cross-legged on Grammy's bed, waiting.

'Quick then, girls,' said Grammy to me and Freya.

'Hurry *up*!' whined Deedee.

Freya perched on the end of Grammy's bed and I sat down on the sheepskin rug on the floor.

'Ready?' Grammy said at last.

We were ready.

Grammy opened the doors of her big cupboard. She lifted out piles of blankets, flannel petticoats and long winter undies, then she pushed aside the clothes that hung on the rail, drawing them back like curtains to reveal the treasure that was hidden behind.

Grammy's secret library.

The sun streamed in through the window, bright as fire, and it lit up the gold on the spine of each book. It lit up the cobwebs that hung all dusty between the black beams above us. It lit up Grammy too – our lovely Grammy – short and strong and wrapped in shawls, her long white hair hanging over her shoulder in a thick plait, her amber eyes glittering with mischief.

'Now, it's been a while since last time, girls,' Grammy said, 'so you'll have to remind me who's readin' what.'

It isn't exactly forbidden to read and write in our village, but the last woman caught reading was given the ducking stool down at Grey Brothers' Pond – twenty times up and down: *splosh*, *GASP*, *splosh*, *GASP*, until all the learning had been washed off her. Grammy says it used to be even worse – her friend Nell's great-grammy kept books, and folks said she was a witch. Blamed her for a bad harvest one year, and she was burnt for it in the end. Some of the men round here can read a bit – just enough to trade at market or with the smugglers' boats that come to the coast. But no man would ever make a show of it, or folks would look at him sideways, and that's the beginning of a bad end for anyone.

So, no one knows we can read. Even Dolly knows to keep it secret, and she's silly as a goose.

One by one we picked our books. We knew Grammy's library well. Many of the books were home-made – handwritten by Mammer and Grammy, and Grammy's mother too – some books she had in-herited, or bought in back rooms by lamplight. She had gathered these treasures secretly over the years and squirrelled them away for us.

Freya was reading a book about pirates – I think it must have had lots of exciting bits, because from time to time she went purple holding her breath. The triplets were reading a book Mammer had written –

Tales of the Marshes (well, Darcy was reading it aloud in a gruff whisper while Dolly and Deedee sat motionless, listening round-mouthed to stories about bog trolls and marsh mermaids).

Grace shook her head when Grammy offered her the book she had been reading. 'I don't feel like it today, Grammy,' she said quietly. 'I'll keep watch for Dadder.' And she turned back to the window.

'Here you are, Willa,' Grammy said, and gave Grace's book to me. My sister had told me about it the last time we read together: it was a story about a princess who doesn't want to be a princess at all – she wants to be a dancer. I opened it up at a picture of the girl dancing at a royal ball, with her dress swirling in the air, red and gold like a setting sun. It was just the right sort of book for Grace; music is in her soul – she loves to sing, and to dance. In the springtime, she dances with flowers in her hair and coloured ribbons all flying behind her; in the winter, she dances wearing a crown of holly, chasing her shadow around and around the Yule Fires. Grace is very well named, I think – when she dances, it's like watching the summer wind shimmer through a hayfield.

Grammy says names are very important. I was named Willa because Grammy says I had a strong will from the moment I was born: I was a fat little babby and loud as a crow – Grammy says I did nothing but scream for two whole years. They had to swaddle me tightly or I wouldn't have slept a wink, and neither would anyone else in the village.

Freya means 'noble lady', which is about right, because she's a bit uppity and thinks very highly of herself. Dolly and Deedee are short for Dolores and Deidre, which both mean sadness, because Mammer died giving birth to them. Everyone thought they were twins, and then little black-haired Darcy slithered out too. Her name means darkness.

Father said Darcy was never a babby at all: she was a demon that grew in Mammer and killed her, and he would have drowned her in the well like a runt puppy if Grammy hadn't stopped him. He still thinks Darcy is jinxed, and he hates me too, though I don't know why. Perhaps because we're the two who favour Mammer's side of the family. The others are all fair like him – summer-blue eyes and hair like ripe corn.

I remember looking at that picture of the dancing princess in Grammy's book that morning and trying to enjoy this rare, precious moment – to let myself drift off to a world far beyond the Lost Marsh, to let the words spark wildfires in my head – but I couldn't concentrate, not with Grace feeling so sad. I'd never seen her sit so still – all huddled up like there was a storm raging around her and she was trying to keep it out. Grammy was watching her too. She sat down beside her and opened a cloth-bound book I knew very well, called *Horses of the Wild* – it was one of my favourites. 'Your Mammer wrote this book when she was about your age, Grace,' Grammy said softly. 'Did all the drawings too.' Grace didn't open it, but she stroked the cloth cover with her fingertips. A tear shone on her cheek.

It was so quiet in Grammy's little sunshiny room. The whisper of pages turning; a mouse rustling in the thatch just a few feet above our heads; Darcy's low voice murmuring about a monstrous marsh king . . . And then Grace started to cry properly – little sniffy shivers at first, and then big, gulping sobs that took the breath out of her. We all looked up from our books. Grammy didn't say a word. She put her arm around Grace's shoulder and squeezed her close. She kissed her gramdaughter's golden hair. Grace sobbed and sobbed into Grammy's shoulder.

I couldn't bear it any longer. 'Dadder can't force Grace to marry Mister Kirby if she doesn't want to, can he?' I said. '*You* got to choose who you married, didn't you, Grammy? And Mammer too?'

'Grace has to marry Silas because of the curse, Willa,' said Deedee with a sigh, as if I were stupid.

'Because of the Curse of Six Daughters,' Dolly echoed, shaking her curls at me. 'Be sure the first girl marries well—'

'Don't,' I said, my guts cramping at the familiar words.

'The second in the home to dwell.'

'Stop it.' But there was no stopping them. Dolly and Deedee were chanting the curse as if it were nothing more than a nursery rhyme. They didn't understand it yet – that feeling, like being caught in a snare, or sucked down into the mire: all your choices already chosen. Dadder thought of it as a curse upon *him*, but it wasn't. Not really. It was a curse upon *us*.

'A third maid can do little harm if set to work upon the farm. Four and five must both be wed, Or six will bury you stone dead.'

We were all silent for a moment. Grace sobbed again.

I shook my head at Dolly and Deedee.

'What?'

'We *know* about the curse,' I said. 'So Grace has to marry well, but why can't she choose *who to*?'

'Because your dadder has decided, that's why,' Grammy said. 'I've tried talking to him, but you know what he's like when it comes to curses and superstitions and such – he won't listen to sense. Silas Kirby is the richest man in the village, and he chose our Grace. Your dadder would never have said no.'

'Well, the curse says *I* have to stay at home,' muttered Freya, frowning down at her book. 'But I'm not going to. I'm going to marry Fergus. I haven't told him yet.'

Fergus Moss is Freya's best friend. He's from a peat-digging family and they live in a cottage out on the bogland.

'The curse says we have to get wed too,' piped up Dolly, and Deedee nodded primly. For them, getting wed was just fairy-tale dresses and pretty flowers. 'Dadder says we've got to be good girls and do what we're told, or the curse will fall upon us, and Darcy will—'

'Yes,' I said. 'We *know*.'

My littlest sister smiled and shrugged, and her dark eyes went back to *Tales of the Marshes*.

What a thing, I thought, *to grow up with that fate hanging over her.*

Grace had turned away from the window and was looking at us all. She had stopped crying now.

Grammy gave her another squeeze. 'Hm?' she said into Grace's hair. 'Don't despair, Gracie. Don't give up, and don't let yourself be druv. You're your own woman, you know. We'll think of something. I promise.'

Grace wiped her eyes on her pinny. 'There's nothing to be done about it, Grammy,' she murmured. 'It's bin decided: I'm to marry Silas at the Springtide Fires. And now Dadder and Silas have gone to the alehouse, the whole village will know about it.'

Grammy opened her mouth to say something, but Grace put her hand on top of Grammy's and shook her head. 'Let's look at the horse book again, please, Grammy,' she said.

Slowly, we all drifted back into our books. The pages whispered once more, the mouse scrabbled in the thatch, and the sunlight moved across the white-washed wall.

In the end it was a noise that jolted us out of our stories. The familiar clunk of the farmyard gate, followed by the scuffing of heavy boots across the yard.

Freya leapt from the bed; I jumped to my feet, heart thumping. Grace twisted to look out of the window.

'He's back! *Quick*, everyone!'

3

Sometimes, at bedtime, the triplets play a very silly game called Bats in the Night. They close the door and curtains, blow out the candles, and they all stand up on their beds. Then they spread out their arms and leap from bed to bed, flapping their wings and squeaking and trying not to crash into each other in the pitch black. As far as I can tell, the winner of the game is the one who doesn't end up on the floor with a bumped head and a bloody nose.

They played Bats in the Night that evening – the same day that Dadder had come home from the alehouse all woolly with grog, and we'd had to rush to hide the books back in Grammy's cupboard. We had forgotten about the soup simmering away in the heavy-bottomed pan, and Freya and I flew down to the kitchen to rescue it just as Dadder staggered up the steps.

Grace stayed upstairs in Grammy's room, as she didn't want Dadder to see she'd been crying, but Dadder was too addled to even notice she wasn't there. I saved a bowl of soup and a lump of bread for Grace, hiding them inside a cooking pot on the hearth to keep warm.

The afternoon went by as usual. I checked on the sheep in the top field, and went with Freya to get water from the well – there and back three times, gripping the buckets with wind-bitten fingers. Then I groomed the horses. Dear old Jet lifted his hooves politely and let me get all the muddy tangles out of his tail, but Flint wouldn't stand still. He wheeled around every time I lifted the brush to his coat.

'Do you want to look nice or not?' I snapped at last. 'You'll get sore feet if you don't let me clean them.'

Flint wouldn't look at me, but he did stand still after that, and when Freya and the triplets trooped past the stable, they gawked and cooed through the door. 'What a beautiful boy!' Dolly exclaimed.

'Bright as a star!' cried Deedee.

Flint lifted his neck handsomely.

'Look at him, with his nose in the air,' Freya said. 'He's too proud by half.'

'Aye, he's proud all right,' I said. 'And stubborn too.'

'And maybe a bit frightened?' said Darcy quietly.

I looked at her, then looked at Flint. I banged the dust out of the grooming brushes.

'I'll tell you exactly what he is,' said Freya over her shoulder, heading for the kitchen door. 'He's a trophy for Dadder. That's what he is.'

I followed the others into the farmyard, bolting the bottom half of the stable door behind me. Then I turned and looked back at Flint – this gleaming, proud, frightened creature who still wouldn't look at me. *He's payment*, I thought. *Payment for our Grace*. And my skin prickled with anger at the whole horrid business.

I helped Freya make dinner, mashing my anger into the potatoes. We mixed in cabbage and sausage meat, and cooked the patties on a hot griddle.

By the time we'd cleaned the kitchen and the triplets had gone up to bed, us older ones were half-asleep ourselves. We sat at the table, our chins on our arms. Dadder snored in his chair by the fire. That was when the thudding began – the thudding and shrieking and squashed laughter of the triplets playing Bats in the Night.

Dadder snorted awake and glared up at the ceiling. Another almighty thud, and dust fell from the beams. '*Darcy*,' he growled.

Dadder always blames Darcy when the triplets are up to mischief. He rarely says her name out loud, but when he does it's like he's spitting out a bit of gristle. The rest of the time he just ignores her. I don't know how anyone can ignore Darcy. She is quiet, but her dark eyes burn with cleverness.

'That girl's the curse on this family,' Dadder slurred. 'She made it six. *She* brought the curse upon us.'

'Nonsense, Nate,' Grammy said firmly. She was sitting in the other fireside chair, knitting mittens for the triplets. 'That curse is nonsense. I wish you'd cast the wretched thing out of your head.'

'No more nonsense than all your stories.'

Grace, Freya and I looked at each other. *Did Dadder know about Grammy's secret library?*

'Lot of rubbish you tell those girls – I've heard you. Tales you tell 'em here by the fire when you think I'm asleep . . .

No – he wasn't talking about her books, thank goodness.

'Or when you put the little ones to bed and hold their paws like they're still babbies. I heard you telling 'em a story 'bout a wolf and three piggywigs . . .'

'Stories are different, Nate . . .'

'You blether on telling your piggywig stories, and then have the nerve to say the Curse of Six Daughters is nonsense?'

'The Curse of Six Daughters *is* nonsense, Nate. Superstitions do us harm – they bind us up with fear.'

Dadder shook his head, but Grammy was right –

you could see the fear in him. Dadder came from a pedlar family. He grew up travelling the Lost Marsh, selling pots and pans, playing music in alehouses with his dadder. His mammer gathered wild herbs to sell on market days. Dadder might like to think he has escaped all that, that he can play the part of a proper farmer now, but superstition is in his blood.

'The tales I tell the girls are different,' Grammy went on. 'Even when they are made up, stories are full of truth. Stories are the places where we learn and feel and dream . . .'

I looked at Grace and saw she had tears in her eyes. What was happening to *her* feelings, *her* dreams? She blinked the tears away quickly.

'Well, there'll be no more silly stories in this house,' Dadder said roughly, jerking his head towards us at the table. 'These dollops can *learn* and *feel* and *dream* as much as they like while they put the chickens away and scrub the floor. And if I say they have to get marrid, then they have to get marrid. A sixth daughter curses a family . . .'

'The only thing cursing this family is your temper, Nate Fernsby – crotchety as a foul old ram you are.'

Dadder's mouth tightened up, all angry, but he didn't shout at Grammy like he would have done at one of us. Dadder has always been a bit afraid of her, and it isn't just because it's her farm, her money. I know some of the other folks in the village feel a bit afraid of her too. It's the way she looks you dead in the eye and says exactly what she thinks. You have to tread carefully in Hollow-in-the-Marsh, though – it's enough to have a bit of respect. You don't want folks to get proper frightened of you . . .

'I'll tell you what it is,' Grammy went on, still calmly stitching. 'It's because it rhymes, isn't it? Folk think that makes it sound all wise and ancient, but any old clod can make up a rhyme. Doesn't make it into a curse or a spell. Doesn't make it true, Nate.'

Freya, Grace and I were watching them, riveted. Our eyes went back and forth, back and forth, checking to see how each word changed the set of Dadder's face. Freya was going purple again with the suspense of it. *Was Dadder listening to Grammy for once? Could this put an end to Grace's betrothal? Or was Grammy pushing him too far?*

Mischief danced in Grammy's eyes; she pointed a wrinkled finger at Dadder: 'If a farmer's tall and pale, his sheep will die, his corn will fail!'

'Quiet, woman,' Dadder snarled, his face growing livid.

'A man who's angry, loud and cruel shall mend his ways on the ducking stool!'

Dadder was fuming mad now. He got to his feet. I don't know what he was about to do, but he was stopped by another loud thud and shriek from upstairs, swiftly followed by a giggled, 'Sssh!'

He looked up. And I went all cold. What Dadder wanted to do was lash out at Grammy, but the triplets were easier prey. *Darcy* was easier prey.

4

I got to my feet. 'I'll go, Dadder,' I said, making
sure I reached the foot of the stairs before he did.
He stopped and glared at me, his eyes glazed with
rage, just inches from my face. I stood my ground. '*I'll
go.*' I was prepared for him to push me out of the way,
but the grog was heavy in him.

'Ha!' His laugh was flat and mocking. He staggered
back to collapse into his chair. 'Yes, *you* go, Willa,' he
snarled. 'Go to hell, for all I care, the whole rotten lot
of you, an' good riddance!'

I ran up the stairs quickly. '*Quiet*, you lot!' I hissed as
I opened the door. My candlelight found Dolly and
Deedee in a tangled heap on the floor, crying with
laughter, while Darcy bounced up and down on my
bed. 'I'm the Bat Queen, Willa!' she declared.

'Congratulations,' I said, closing the door behind me. 'But you've got to be quiet now, your highness. Dadder heard you, and he'll come up if you make any more noise.'

The bouncing stopped.

'We couldn't sleep,' Deedee whined.

'I don't think you've actually tried,' I huffed. 'Getting into bed would be a start.'

They untangled themselves and clambered into their beds, still breathless. 'Tell us a story, Willa?'

'I'm too tired to think of one,' I said, tucking the blankets tightly around them so they wouldn't be tempted to start leaping about again.

'You don't have to *think* of a story . . .' Darcy whispered, sitting up again suddenly, her eyes all glowy, like little fires.

I knew that look.

She lifted her pillow and pulled out *Tales of the Marshes*.

'Darcy!'

'You can't take books out of Grammy's room!'

'Hide it, quick!'

'What if Dadder finds it?'

'He won't find it.' Darcy shrugged. Sometimes I thought there was nothing in the world that could frighten my littlest sister. 'Read it, Willa,' she said. 'Please?'

I sighed and opened the book at the tale of the

Marsh King. 'Just one story,' I said. 'And you've all got to lie still-as-stone and close your eyes.'

Six bright eyes snapped shut.

'*Beware the dangers of the marsh, my darlings,*' I read, tilting the book into the candlelight so I could make out Mammer's faded, twisty letters, '*beware the mire. Do not lose your way, and never let fear be your guide.*'

Darcy nodded very seriously, her eyes shut tight.

'*Many winters ago, an evil sprite roamed these marshes. He lured folk out into the mire with his will-o'-the-wisp lantern. The marsh folk were afraid of him — afraid that he would use his false flame to ensnare the souls of their loved ones and to steal their livestock.*

'*The evil sprite fed upon their fear — he grew fat and gleeful. He used folks' fears to control them, and the more frightened they were, the stronger he became. He built himself a strange little castle on the mire. He made himself a crown of bones, and he called himself the Marsh King.*

'*There were only two people who did not fear the Marsh King — two sisters called Gloria and Gytha Greenwood. They wrote the Marsh King down in a book — all the wicked things he did, and all his cruel tricks too — as a warning to others.*

'*The Marsh King found out about the book, and it was the first time he had ever known fear himself: he was afraid folk would hunt him down with torches and dogs. So, he used his dark magic. He spread whispers that writing was witchcraft, that the Greenwood sisters were witches. He stirred up fear* and suspicion, until the villagers turned against the Greenwoods and burnt their farmhouse down. The book was destroyed in the blaze, and Gloria Greenwood was killed.

'But the Marsh King didn't stop there. He conjured curses and jinxes, so that folk were too frightened to rise up against him. He whipped up superstitions which blew like dandelion seeds all over the Lost Marsh, and took root wherever they fell. Fear flourished. Folk became afraid of everything – afraid of books and cleverness, magpies and black cats, blood moons and even their own daughters.

'And in this way, the Marsh King ruled over people who were mere shadows of themselves – frightened and cowed. He druv them like sheep, and he druv them like cattle, and they did not question their own misery.

'Young Gytha Greenwood was broken with grief after her sister's death. Folk called her the Sundered Soul.'

'What's sundered, Willa?'

'Sundered means she felt torn apart, ripped down the middle. She would sit night and day by her sister's grave up on the hill, gazing out towards the shadowy mire.

'Months passed. May blossomed and the corn grew tall. Hay swayed in the meadows, ripe for scything. The days lengthened towards midsummer like a dog stretching in the afternoon sun, and the marshes shone like gold.

'On the night of the midsummer moon, Gytha Greenwood set out on to the mire, heading straight towards the light of a mysterious lantern that flickered there. But Gytha had a lantern of her own. She took out her little tin tinderbox and struck a bright, bright flame. Then, all alone, she walked into the darkness.

'*And she was never seen again.*'

'Oh! Did the Marsh King get her?'

'Perhaps – but listen: *The Marsh King was never seen again either. And it wasn't long before his castle crundled down into the mire . . .*'

'Dead, then,' said Deedee.

'Good,' nodded Dolly.

'Ah – defeated, p'raps, but not dead,' whispered Grammy's voice from the doorway. None of us had heard her come in. She smiled, waiting for her breath to catch up with her after climbing the stairs. 'A magical being is not as easy to destroy as all that,' she said at last. 'Especially one as cruel and cunning as the Marsh King.'

'What happened to him, then?' asked Darcy. 'Where did he go?'

'It's just a story, Darcy,' Deedee murmured, half-asleep now.

'Just a story,' echoed Dolly, as she turned over and started snoring very softly.

Grammy closed the door behind her and came to sit on Darcy's bed with me. She looked at the book and smiled.

'Your mammer wrote this not long after you were born, Willa.'

She stroked the lovely, hand-painted lettering on

the cover, and my fingertips followed hers. *Mammer's hands made this.*

'Ah,' Grammy sighed. 'I'd better put it away now.' She took *Tales of the Marshes* gently from my hands and stood up. 'I'll keep it safe.'

'Where *did* the Marsh King go, Grammy?' Darcy asked, sitting up.

'Well, some say a wisp of his spirit still wanders the Lost Marsh, hiding here and there, sniffing out fear and despair, luring lost souls to their doom with his false flame. That's why it's so important not to lose your way on the mire, and to know the difference between a will-o'-the-wisp and a true light.'

Darcy harrumphed and lay down again, cross that the magic of the fairy tale had given way to one of Grammy's sensible lessons. 'Someone should stop that Marsh King,' she muttered.

'Yes, my darling.' Grammy tucked her in and kissed her cheek. 'Another brave being. Another sundered soul, p'raps. Now sleep tight. Don't let the marsh bugs bite. Dream of nice things.'

'I will, Grammy,' Darcy murmured. And she fell asleep with a fierce scowl on her face, like she was setting off through her dreams to hunt down the mythical Marsh King and slay him at last.

5

The Full Moon Fayre arrived the next morning, along with the first snowfall of winter. The clouds hung heavy in the sky like the belly of a great beast and, not long after breakfast, the first snowflakes fell — floating to the earth, light as thistledown, impossibly white.

From the top field, Grace, Freya and I watched teams of night-black horses pulling carts, caravans and wagons down the narrow lane to our village — the fresh snow was soon churned to an ankle-deep slush of mud and horse muck.

They set up the fayre on Silas Kirby's biggest meadow, right on the edge of the mire. The tents were a hundred different colours, sizes and shapes. From where we were standing, it looked as if someone had emptied Grammy's bag of sewing scraps on to the snowy field. The biggest tent was in the middle – red-and-white striped, with flags on top like a castle.

'Oh! It's just how I remember!' Grace gasped. 'That's where we saw the tumblers and the dancers, and the horses all in a circle, and the girl like a silver arrow in the air!' My sister's face was shining.

No one knows when the Full Moon Fayre will come. It might as well be called the Blue Moon Fayre, Grammy says. Sometimes it comes twice a season, and then not for years and years. The only time we'd ever been to the fayre was ten years ago, when Mammer was still alive – Grace was six and Freya was five. I can't remember it at all – I was only two.

'You sat on Mammer's lap when we watched the tumblers,' Freya said. 'I remember because you took my toffee apple and it got all stuck in Mammer's hair.'

'What's in all the other tents?' I asked.

'Lots of things! Fortune tellers, jugglers, sword-swallowers and fire-eaters, mimes, magic shows – and food like you've never tasted before!'

I was trembling with excitement: 'D'you think Dadder will let us go?'

'Not tonight,' Dadder said, when Grace asked him later that day.

It was 'not tonight' all week. Every evening we watched the moon rise, waxing bigger and fuller;

every evening we watched the bobbing lanterns move through the village as folk flocked to the fayre. And then it was the night of the full moon. The fayre always stayed until the full moon – ending with a spectacular show – and then it was gone by morning.

This was our last chance . . .

'All right. You big ones can go,' Dadder grunted.

The three of us whooped and leapt in the air. 'Not you, Willa,' he said in a low voice. 'Grace and Freya can go. You've been a pox of late. Your nonsense might've scuppered Grace's betrothal.'

'But, Dadder, that's not fair, I—'

'I said NO,' he thundered. 'Grace and Freya can go to the fayre, and you can do their jobs for them. Have you bin up to the top field today?'

My hands clenched into fists. 'Not yet . . .' How dare he try to catch me out like that? Most of the time he had no idea what was happening on the farm. But he was right. The sheep needed hay in this weather.

So, while Grace and Freya scrubbed their faces and put on their best skirts and twisted each other's hair into ringlets, I wrapped myself in a heavy shawl and trudged through the snow up to our sheep field. Darcy came with me – she knew how disappointed and cross I was, and having her there by my side like a little skipping shadow made me feel a bit better. We took the barrow to carry the hay bale, wheeling it carefully across the plank bridging the frozen ditch. Then we heaved the hay out into the field. Most of the grass was stiff with ice or covered in snow and the sheep were hungry. They crowded round us – warm and damp, their woolly coats steaming. While they golloped down the hay, we felt their tums for any signs of lambs starting. They'd been put to the ram some weeks before. We'd had to separate the flock for this. Our old sheepdog Bess had died the year before, and there had been no new litters of pups in the village, so the triplets scampered around the field instead, weaving this way and that way, crouching on their haunches and darting about, pretending to be sheepdogs and herding the ewes into a pen.

'Lots of twins come spring, I think,' I said, gently feeling the tum of one of the younger ewes.

Darcy nodded. 'Aye. Dadder will be pleased.'

I walked to the water trough and used a big stone to shatter the ice into hard white blades . . . *Dadder*.

Darcy watched me. 'You could go to the fayre anyway,' she said quietly. 'I won't tell.'

I kicked at the trough, thinking about it. It wouldn't be easy. Dadder slept in a box bed near the kitchen fire, and he wasn't always as grogged up as he'd been after Grace's betrothal. I thought about how angry he'd been with me earlier – calling me a pox. If he caught me disobeying him, I'd be in for a whipping, or a night in the stables. But then I thought about all those brightly coloured tents and the magic and secrets they contained . . . Tonight was the last night of the fayre, and who knew when it would next be back?

Could I find a way of sneaking out?

I brushed the cobwebs from the corners and mopped the kitchen floor. I tied a broom to a long pole and swept the snow from the roof so it wouldn't soak through the thatch. I sharpened the knives and polished the pans until they shone. When I told Dadder that the lambing looked promising, he didn't look at me, but he nodded and said, 'Ar. P'raps you'll be useful yet, Willa Fernsby.'

I smiled sweetly. I thought about bobbing an obedient curtsy, but I thought that might be overdoing it a bit.

Grace and Freya were ready at last. They trotted downstairs, all bright skirts and gleaming curls, and went to kiss Grammy goodbye. She was sitting beside the fire, mending a thick dress that had already done for Grace, Freya and me, and was now being altered for Dolly: patched up like an old prize fighter so that it might return to the ring. Grammy rummaged in the bottom of her scraps bag and pulled out some shiny coins. Dadder was just a few yards away – standing by the door, polishing his riding boots. Grammy checked he wasn't looking, then she winked and passed the coins to Grace, who shoved them in her pocket. The flames in the kitchen fire frolicked about like merry demons.

'I remember my first trip to the Full Moon Fayre,' Grammy said wistfully. 'The music, the colours, the costumes, the food! . . . I had my fortune told by a twisty old hag who scared the days out of me.'

'Did it come true?' Grace asked. 'What she said?'

Grammy thought for a moment. 'Now let me see . . . Yes, I believe it did. She told me I'd marry a good man who'd die young, and she said I'd end up with six rag-a-tag gramdaughters.'

Freya gasped. 'Did she really say that?'

'Well, maybe not the last bit.' Grammy's eyes twinkled and she turned to look at me polishing the last copper pan at the kitchen table. 'I couldn't have been much older than you, Willa. The fayre turned up at Lammas – harvest time – and I was twelve, because I had my pup Thunder with me and he was my birthday present.' Her eyes clouded over. 'My Thunder . . .'

We had heard the story a hundred times before – the sheepdog pup Grammy had adored, *fierce and loyal and black as a storm cloud*. Darcy loved hearing about Thunder more than any of us. As a tot, she was so taken with Grammy's tales about him that he became her imaginary pet. She would throw sticks for him, and take him for brisk walks around the farmyard. She talked to him in her sleep sometimes, patting the blanket next to her and murmuring, 'Here, Thunder. Good pup . . .'

'Thunder ran away, the night I visited the Full Moon

Fayre,' Grammy said sadly. 'Must've got lost out on the mire.'

'P'raps the Marsh King got him,' Darcy piped up. She was sitting on the stairs, listening.

Grammy smiled sadly. 'Well. He never came home.'

Grace bent to kiss Grammy gently on her snow-white head. 'He was a good pup.'

'He was.' Grammy sniffed back the tears. 'Oh, but that was long ago. Well, don't let me stop your fun. Be good lasses, now, won't you?'

Grace nodded and Freya squeezed Grammy's hand.

'And make sure you stick together. That's the only rule. Stick together.'

I waved at Grace and Freya as they left, making sure my face looked jealous, and not at all like I was plotting something.

There was a slight movement on the stairs, and I saw Darcy's eyes shining there in the darkness.

'Get to bed, *you*,' Dadder growled at her. He had finished polishing his boots now and was opening a bottle of grog. 'And tell those other silly whelps to get to bed too.'

'N'night, Dadder,' she said.

Dadder just grunted, turning his back on her and collapsing into his comfy chair with the bottle in his hand.

Darcy moved up a step or two, then stopped and turned around again. In her arms was something that looked like a blanket, all bundled up. She opened her eyes wide and nodded at me. It was time.

I filled myself up with a big, brave breath. 'Think I'll go up to bed with the triplets, Dadder. I'll make sure they don't start any nonsense.'

'Ar. Night, then,' and he swigged from his bottle.

'N'night, Darcy. N'night, Willa,' said Grammy.

I went up the stairs after Darcy. Then I turned back and said the words I had been practising in my head. I hoped they sounded real, and not too much like lumps of cheese to bait a mousetrap: 'Dadder, when I looked in on Flint tonight, I thought he looked a bit bloated. D'you think he's bin eating all Jet's oats?'

Dadder sat up straight as a poker. 'Flint?' Grog sloshed on to the flagstones as he set the bottle down on the hearth and, before I knew it, he was halfway to the door. 'Not the colic. Not Flint,' he muttered. 'It's that *curse*, I swear . . .' And he hurried out into the night.

Darcy was still there a few steps above me. 'Go, Willa!' she breathed, throwing me the bundle she was holding. It unfurled in mid-air into a beautiful blue cloak. I wrapped it quickly around my shoulders and pulled up the hood. Darcy nodded, giving me her serious little salute. 'Thank you,' I grinned. I ran back down the stairs and through the kitchen, kissing my startled grammy on the way. I followed Dadder's shadow through the kitchen door and out into the yard. I waited until he was inside the stable with his back to me, still chuntering away about the curse, holding up his lantern to examine a perfectly lean and healthy horse; then I ran on through the snow – silent as a cat – to catch up with Grace and Freya on the lane.

6

'You can't come with us, Willa,' Freya whined when I finally caught up with them. 'We'll *all* be for it if Dadder finds out!' But I knew she was just cross that I was barging in on their evening; she had been looking forward to having Grace all to herself. 'And what are you wearing? Is that Mammer's cloak?'

'I don't know – Darcy gave it to me.'

'It was Mammer's,' Grace said quietly, taking an edge of the cloak between her gloved fingers. It was a deep, deep, shimmering blue. She smiled gently. 'It suits you, Willa – you should keep it.' Then she got herself between me and Freya, hooked her arms around us both and marched us onward. 'C'mon. Let's go to the fayre!'

The way through the village was bright with

lanterns and all sleety and airey as the winter wind whipped about us. I hardly felt the cold at all, though. I was lit up inside like a baker's oven.

From the moment we stepped into the colourful chaos of the fayre, the salty-stagnant smell of the marshland was displaced by smells of slow-roasted meat, baked apples, spiced batter frying in hot pans. My tum groaned loudly.

'What about a baked apple each?'

And so the three of us went to the nearest apple stall, hand in hand like paper dolls.

I had never tasted anything like those apples in all my life; none of us had. We huddled up in a dark space between the tents, scoffing like piglets, and we didn't say a word until the last hot, sweet mouthfuls had disappeared down our throats.

'What now?' Grace asked, breathless.

'How about the show? The tumblers and dancers!'

'Yes,' said Grace, with shining eyes.

'*Yes!*' Freya grabbed my hand and set off, almost galloping towards the big tent, giddy as a goat. I was glad she had forgotten about not wanting me with them. The ecstasy of this moment – running through the fayre with my sisters, the winter night above us and the bright lanterns all around, the warm sweetness of the spiced apple in my tum, the dizzy, swimmy feeling of unknowable adventures ahead – I had never felt joy quite like it.

'Look!' Grace called out as we all capered along. 'A fortune teller – just like Grammy said!'

She was hanging back now, looking at a tent with a gold-fringed doorway. The light inside was wine-red, dangerous and irresistible. I caught a glimpse of the fortune teller – not a twisty old hag like Grammy had said, but a young woman with auburn hair, all in red, her wrists heavy with gold. I wanted to stop too, but Freya had let go of my hand and was already too far ahead; I didn't want to lose her in the crowd. 'After the show, Grace – come *on*! The *dancers*, Grace!'

I was aware of heading into the very heart of things, through circles of food tents, past jugglers and fiddlers – deeper and deeper into the fayre. I felt fit to burst with the jigging inside me – the lights and the smells and the wonder of it all. The big red-and-white striped tent glowed and pulsed with music. As we approached the entrance, the silk doors drew magically back, gathered up by scarlet ropes.

We paid our money to a young fella with black hair that flopped over his eyes. He took the coins from Grace's hand, and waved us all through the silk doors. 'Enjoy the show, ladies!' he grinned, and we all went in, gaping with anticipation.

Inside, it was almost hot. All the villagers were crowded in together, their faces lit by hundreds of full-moon paper lanterns that swayed on invisible strings around us. This was the last night of the fayre – this was the spectacular Full Moon Show! In the middle of the tent was a round space covered with wood-shavings. The six night-black horses that had pulled the wagons through the village were cantering in a circle, perfectly in time, while six elfin children balanced on their backs playing drums.

There was a sudden crash of noise and a cloud of smoke. Freya shrieked, but when I looked at her she was all gleeful, her eyes big and not blinking in case she missed a second of it. When the smoke cleared, a man was standing in the middle of the ring. He was wearing a top hat and a long purple coat, and he had a huge white tiger at his side. *A tiger!* I'd heard of them, of course, I'd seen them in pictures, but they'd been no more real to me than dragons or sea monsters. To have one right here, just yards away – with real claws and real teeth . . .

The man cracked a whip, and the tiger roared. The night-black horses all reared up, spun on their hind hooves and stamped down, stopping dead. Everyone in the audience was staring, mouths open like carp. The man raised his arms in the sudden silence.

'Ladies and gentlemen, boys and girls,' he shouted. 'Welcome to the FULL! MOON! FAYRE!'

Then the tent erupted with noise – blaring trumpets, thumping drums and the clapping and cheering of the crowd. Fifty performers poured into the ring, tumbling, cartwheeling, breathing fire. Dancers dressed as swans swung back and forth over the stage on fine ropes, their feather-white costumes streaming out behind them.

There were animals being paraded around in glittering collars – animals I'd only ever seen before in Grammy's books: an elephant, a bear, a zebra. The white tiger sat in the middle of the ring, roaring and dabbing at the air with her huge white paws every time the man in purple snapped at the leash. The animals were so extraordinary and so beautiful, but I hated to see them like that – wild creatures yoked and whip-driven: it felt wrong. I wanted to let them loose into the Lost Marsh, but then I worried that the tiger would eat all the sheep, and it would be too cold for the elephant. I turned to say this to Grace – I felt sure she would feel the same way about the animals – but the seat beside me was empty.

Grace was not there.

'Freya, where's Grace?'

'Hmm?' Freya was entranced.

'Where's Grace gone?'

She shrugged. 'Probably just gone to get another apple or something. Go and look for her if you're worried.'

So I went, pushing my way back through the crowd and ducking beneath the scarlet curtains, back past the boy with the floppy black hair, and out into the cold night.

47

7

There! A figure in the gloom, willowy and swift, the curls of her hair shining like jewels in the coloured lights.

'Grace!' I shouted, trying to make her hear me above the music and cheering that erupted from the big tent. '*Grace!*'

But she was running away from me.

I followed her into the dark maze of tents, twisting and turning through the silken corridors that reeked of tobacco smoke and foreign spices. A large brown rat scurried across my path. A monkey screamed from the shoulder of a juggler; a giant man challenged people to arm-wrestle him and win a barrel of rum. He was roaring and lunging at the crowd; his bare arms bulged with muscle. A painted clown face leered at me from nowhere – 'Penny for the show, miss?' he shrieked, raising his hat and releasing a bird that exploded into the air above me. I rushed past them all, ignoring my drumming heart and trying to keep my sister in sight. I thought of Grammy's words: *Stick together. That's the only rule. Stick together . . .*

But we had come unstuck.

What was Grace doing? Why was she running away? She seemed to be heading right through the fayre and out the other side, running towards the far edge of the meadow. There were only a few scattered tents left between us and the edge of Hollow Mire . . .

'*Grace!*' I called again, and this time she stopped and turned.

'Oh, Grace! What's wrong? What is it?' My sister's face – so sparkly-bright when we arrived at the fayre – was red with crying. She was breathless, tears coursing down her cheeks. 'Grace?' I grabbed her wrists. 'Tell me – what happened?'

'The fortune teller,' she gasped at last.

'What about the fortune teller?'

But Grace's eyes fixed on something behind me. 'Oh, no . . .'

I turned quickly and saw Silas Kirby and another man from the village sauntering along the edge of the fayre towards us. Silas laughed loudly. 'No, *you* wrestle the giant, Bill,' he guffawed, slapping the other man on the back. 'I'll pay double to watch him snap your arm in two!'

'Help me, Willa,' Grace begged. 'I don't want him to see me.'

'This way.' I tugged her through the door of the nearest tent and we held our breath as the two men went past.

'Has he gone?'

I poked my head back through the gap. 'He's gone.'

'Did he see us?'

'I don't think so.'

Grace took a long shaking breath. We both turned into the tent, pushing through the curtains, layers of cool white silk brushing our hands and our faces, until we were safely inside.

'Sit down, Grace,' I said, leading her to a row of empty chairs. The little tent appeared to be ready for some sort of performance. A set of tattered theatre curtains hung in front of a small stage. An old round lantern swung from the silken ceiling, the flame inside flickering warmly. It was all quiet, and we were the only people in there. I passed Grace a handkerchief and gave her a moment to mop her face.

'What did the fortune teller say, Grace? Was it about Silas?'

Grace nodded, and her breath came quickly as she swallowed down another sob.

'I went in – I only went in because I thought she was

bound to say somethin' nice, somethin' comforting, like Grammy was told when she was young. I just wanted to hear someone say I'd have a happy marriage; that he would turn out to be a good man . . .'

'But she didn't say that?'

'No.' Grace was staring at her hands, clenched into fists in her lap. 'She looked at my palm and she didn't say anything at all. She just went all pale. Then she checked the other palm. Then she tried the cards . . .'

'An act, Grace – it's just part of the show. That's how they make their money. They want it to be all dramatic . . .'

Grace shook her head. She opened a fist and showed me a gleaming silver coin. 'She gave me my money back. And she told me to run.'

A cold shiver went right through me. '*Run?*'

Grace nodded. 'She said, *Run – it's not too late, child – you might still escape your fate.*'

'Oh, Grace . . .'

I put my arms around my big sister and hugged her tightly. After a while I drew back to look at her face. I tucked a damp curl behind her ear and tried to smile. 'The fortune teller said it's not too late, didn't she? So perhaps we can talk to Dadder – he actually believes in curses and this sort of thing, so it might change his mind if you tell him . . .'

But then there was a rustling noise behind the tattered curtains and a small, hunched man climbed through. He smiled at us and spread out his hands. 'Welcome!' he said.

The man wore a scarecrow hat; his face was all wrinkled, and his grass-green eyes shone with a light like kindness itself. He looked at Grace's face. It was obvious she had been crying. 'Poor soul,' the man said. 'Perhaps my shadow-puppet show will cheer you up? What do you say?'

I looked at Grace. *Shall we?*

She nodded.

The man smiled again. 'It'll get pitchy dark now, girls,' he said, reaching into the old lantern to pinch out the flame. 'But only for a moment. Hold tight!'

Suddenly we were both sitting there in the darkness. My face was only inches away from my sister's, but I could not see her at all. Everything was black — deep, underground black. I closed my eyes and opened them again: it was exactly the same.

There was a shuffling sound and a waft of old cloth as the man in the scarecrow hat went back through the theatre curtains. Pinpricks of light began twinkling above us — stars in the night sky, and then a soft glow started to fill the tent. The tattered curtains opened very slowly, jerking on their runners.

Behind them was a sort of screen, like a great silk sheet. It blushed with light, and then, from all around us, came the thin, piping notes of a kingfisher.

'We shouldn't stay for long,' I whispered to Grace.

'We should go and find Freya . . .'

'Let's just stay for a minute,' she said in a low voice, bewitched by the magic of it. 'It's so beautiful.'

Shadows of reeds and bulrushes were becoming distinct on the screen – black silhouettes against the warming light: sunset over the marsh. A full moon hung pale and perfect in the silken sky. The kingfisher appeared then – or rather, the shadow of a kingfisher puppet. It darted through the reeds, swift as an arrow. This was like no puppet show I had ever seen before. This was magical. As more birds and creatures appeared on the screen, I became aware that, beneath my warm cloak and thick winter dress, my arms were covered in goosebumps. I wasn't watching a puppet show any more – I was there on the marsh, watching the sun set, surrounded by birds ruffling their wet feathers and otters splashing in the reeds. I saw a fisherman cast his line into a rippling pool, a little dog sitting patiently at his side.

Starlings flocked above the marsh in a swirling murmuration – a hypnotic shadow shape that dipped and twisted and swelled and soared – now a cloud, now a great eagle, now a beckoning hand, now a girl dancing . . . And then there were great waves rising and falling beneath the birds – we were flying over oceans, over forests, over mountains! It was a glorious dream of light and hope and freedom, and I felt myself drawn into it as if into a blissful sleep.

I don't know how long the show went on for. When the shadows faded away and the lantern flickered once more, Grace and I blinked at each other. Here we were, back in the tattered little tent. Grace looked more like herself now – that smile was back in her eyes.

'Beautiful,' she said.

'Let's go and find Freya,' I said, and Grace nodded.

We got up from our chairs and went towards the door where the shadowman was already waiting. He took off his scarecrow hat and held it out politely. Grace dropped in the silver coin that the fortune teller had given back to her.

'That was a wonderful show,' she said.

The shadowman smiled and bowed. 'Thank 'ee, girls.'

8

W e found Freya at the baked-apple stall, talking to the boy with the floppy black hair. She looked furious when she saw us. 'Where have you *been*?' she snapped. 'We've been looking everywhere! I was just about to go home without you. Then you'd've been in for it – *both* of you.'

'Sorry, Freya,' Grace said, smothering her sister's rage with a hug. 'We weren't gone for long.'

'You've been gone *ages*,' came the muffled reply.

'Sorry, Freya,' I said. 'We stopped and saw a show – we must have lost track of time.'

'You missed the dancers, Grace,' Freya said, ignoring me. 'They were wonderful! You'd have loved them!' She turned to the boy with the black hair. 'My sister Grace is a *very* good dancer, Viktor.'

'A dancer, is she?' said Viktor. He looked at Grace in that way young men often do. He pushed his floppy hair off his face, and stood up a bit taller. 'Well, the big show is one performer short at the moment. My father has been trying to find a new dancer for months now. He's the showman – the one with the purple suit, and the tiger.'

We all nodded. Freya folded her arms, pleased with herself for finding such an important new friend.

'Would you like to run away with the fayre, Miss Grace?' Viktor smiled. He spread his arms out to embrace the world around him. 'Life as a dancer! Travelling with us far and wide!'

Grace looked at him for a moment, as if trying to judge if he was serious or not.

A dancer! I pictured my sister dressed in one of the beautiful swan costumes, making the crowd gasp as she leapt and flew . . . *To be doing what she loves best. To travel beyond the Lost Marsh, and to have her own money too. To escape the curse and Silas Kirby . . .*

But then Grace smiled politely and shook her head. 'Thank you, Viktor. It was so nice to meet you. And thank you for looking after Freya.'

'He wasn't *looking after* me,' Freya insisted as we went off together through the fayre. 'He was helping me look for *you* two!'

She couldn't stay cross for long, though. Grace

bought us three cups of hot elderberry punch, and we went to see a magic show: a conjuror called Albina the Great, who made a boy disappear from a spinning cupboard and then reappear back in the crowd. I'd never seen anyone like Albina before. She was tall as a giantess – taller even than Dadder. Her hair was white as moonlight, cut close on her head, and she conjured fifty white doves from the sleeve of her shimmering cloak. At the end of the show, she bowed to the crowd, smiled, and then vanished in a sudden puff of smoke.

When we got home, I hid in the henhouse and waited for my sisters to signal that the coast was clear. I waited and waited, and in the end it was Grammy who came out to find me, all wrapped up in winter shawls, with her face peeping out like a hedgehog. 'Your dadder's asleep now, Willa. Come quietly to the door with me and wait for the right moment. And remember the squeaky step on the stairs.'

'Are you afraid of Dadder too, Grammy?' I whispered.

She smiled. 'No, Willa. I'm not afraid of your dadder. But I won't always be here to protect you from his rages, and there's no need to wake a snoozin' bull, is there?'

I caught her arm. 'Grace is afraid of him. And she's afraid of Silas Kirby too. Did she tell you what the fortune teller said? She told her to run away.'

Grammy nodded. 'Aye. I've promised her we'll sort it all out somehow. I said we'll find a way.'

'What did she say?'

'She just gave me a hug.' Grammy smiled.

It snowed again that night. I couldn't sleep and neither could Grace, so we watched the snow together, tumbling down from the blackness in great fluffy tufts. The world outside our bedroom window was shushed and muffled – like someone else's dream. Grace and I shivered side by side in our nighties as the others all slept.

'It's beautiful, Willa,' Grace whispered. 'Look – it's makin' everythin' beautiful.'

'Even the yard,' I said. 'Even the muck pile.'

'Look – Flint is watchin' the snow too.'

I squinted towards the stable – and could just make out the ghostly shape of the horse's head, moving back and forth as if to catch the snowflakes on his velvet nose.

Grace's fingers reached for mine and squeezed them tight.

'What?' I whispered.

She cuddled up to me, all warm. 'Nothing,' she said.

I wish I had known then what I know now – that the next night there would only be five Fernsby girls in that room. I would have hugged my big sister a little bit harder, held on to her hand just a little bit longer.

When morning came, Grace had gone. And the snow had covered her tracks.

PART TWO

Springtide

With the spring tides, the lower fields flood with saltwater. New ditches must be dug. Folk whisper of sea monsters in the bogland, mermaids in the mire. The hawthorn is blossoming now. The earth hums with green growth; fires are lit to welcome the spring . . .

May Fernsby, 'The Marsh Mermaids', *Tales of the Marshes*

9

It has been a whole season since Grace left. Yuletide has come and gone, and the New Year too. The winter was a bitter one. Some folk in the village struggled, but our fields are the highest in the village — beyond the reach of the saltwater floods. We had a good harvest last year, and we still have plenty of hay left for the animals too. When the thaw came at last, we lit candles and thanked the earth for our stocked-up store cupboards and a good lambing. Now the snowdrops have finished, and the bluebells are on their way, pushing up bright fountains of leaves between the shadowy tree roots.

Lying here, on Glorious Hill, I can feel the warmth of spring soaking through the turf. It won't be long until the Springtide Fires. Freya is lying here beside me with her eyes closed against the morning sunshine. The triplets are rolling down the meadow, shrieking and spinning all the way down to the rushy bank of Grey Brothers' Pond.

Today, the five of us are entrusted with the spring promises. We left the farm early to call on the blacksmith and the beekeeper, the saddler, the miller, and Silas Kirby. At each stop, Freya and I pledged a full-grown lamb come weaning, and we were given promises in return – horseshoes for Jet and Flint, a dozen jars of lavender honey, a new saddle, four sacks of flour . . . Silas made no promise to us, of course. He just nodded sourly at our offering of a healthy ewe lamb and a sturdy little ram, then he slammed the door on us. Everyone knows Dadder is in Silas's debt since Grace ran away. The trouble is, Dadder can't bear to part with Flint. Even though Flint leads Dadder a merry dance every time he rides him – skittering and rearing, bucking and bolting – he still loves that horse more than he loves anything in the world. Or at least he loves what Flint makes him look like: a gentleman. Dadder has had a new riding coat made, and his long riding boots are glossy as night.

When Grace disappeared, Dadder started riding out on Flint every day. He swore to Silas he would find his bride and drag her home in time to be wed at the Springtide Fires – it was the only way to keep Silas from taking Flint back again. But it has been three long months now, and there is no sign of Grace anywhere. Dadder still rides out most days, though. 'He's showing that horse off all over the marsh,' Grammy says. 'And he likes to be away from the village. Away from Silas Kirby and the eyes of all the elders, who know him to be a debtor.'

Dadder has sworn to them that Grace will honour the betrothal. He has sworn it on his life. But he is only saying that to keep them off his back. Silas is not known for being a patient or forgiving man.

Our spring promises have brought us all the way through the village: down our high-hedged lane to the lower land of the cottages, where stinking trenches are dug all around to keep the marsh from their doors. We cartwheeled across the village green, and stopped to drink the cold, sweet water from the well. We came past the smart stables of Silas Kirby's farm, across the big meadow where the Full Moon Fayre stood just a few months ago, right on the brink of Hollow Mire, and then across the common land and up on to Glorious Hill. Grammy gave us a picnic for our journey, so here we are lazing on the grass, our tums full of fresh-baked huffkins and cherry jam.

'Funny that it's called Glorious Hill,' Freya murmurs, drowsy with food, fresh air and spring sunshine. 'Everything else around here is called something damp and miserable, like Boggy End or Frog's Bottom.'

I laugh. 'It's called Glorious Hill because it's so glorious.' I pluck at the cool grass with my fingers. I push myself up to take in the view once more – the gentle slope of this grassy hillside, rising up from the marsh like an island, a glimpse of the pond and the old ducking stool through the green-gold willows, the farms and cottages of our village, and then the miles and miles of flat marshland that surround us: grazing fields riddled with drainage ditches; reedy, shimmering wetlands; brown peatbog fading into the pale horizon of the sea; and, all around, in deadly sweeping swathes, the dark grasses of the mire . . .

Around to my right, on the bumpier, more gentle slope of Glorious Hill, there are lots of trees – but it isn't exactly a woodland – it's the closest thing Hollow-in-the-Marsh has to a graveyard. When someone dies, we bury them and plant a tree to mark their resting place. Mammer's tree is here near the top of the rise. It's a sweet chestnut, already two or three times taller than me – its leaves a cool, bright green, its branches broadening with each year that passes. There is a young horse chestnut here too, a bit taller than Mammer's tree and growing just a few yards away. I think this is my favourite place in the world – lying on the warm earth beneath these chestnut trees. I feel peaceful here. I feel whole.

The other trees are mainly our ancestors on Grammy's side of the family: hazel and blackthorn, holly and elm, and an oak for her husband – our grampy who died long before any of us were born. When I die, I should like to be buried under a willow tree, I think. It isn't a ghoulish thought – it's a happy one. It's nice to think of what sort of tree we might become one day. Glorious Hill is a very special place. The sun always seems to shine here. In summer, we swim in the pond, and doze amongst the wild flowers; when the snow comes, we race all the way down the treeless side of the hill on sledges and trays. The upper slope of the meadow is steep enough to get a good, fast start for sledging, or for rolling . . . The triplets are puffing their way back up to us now, dizzy and giggling, covered in grass, and blotted with mud from worm casts.

'Come on, then, everyone,' Freya says, sitting up at last. 'We can't stay here all day.'

Since Grace left, Freya has got a new big-sister voice. She is the oldest now, I suppose, but it still prickles me when she takes that tone, especially as I have bags more common sense than she does. And I don't like her stepping into Grace's shoes . . .

'Sort your hair out, please, Darcy – we don't want to be late. The Mosses are expecting us.'

So we shake the crumbs from the blanket, and Freya wipes jam off the faces of the triplets with the cleanest corner of her pinny, and we get ourselves ready for the last part of our quest – the walk out over the marsh to the peat-diggers' cottage, where Freya's friend Fergus lives with his mammer and dadder, Missus and Mister Moss.

As we walk across the marsh, a skylark bounces up from amongst the green shoots. He trills and burbles high above us – just a little dot in the blue. The pure notes are a spring promise all of their own. We tramp along in a raggedy line, bridging the saltwater ditches with planks that are left here and there. We cross cornfields and sheep fields, until at last we reach the bogland – an expanse of brown turf, square-dug pits and peat-black puddles. The warm, ancient, rotting smell of the earth is cut through with breezes from the sea, bold and brackish.

'This way,' says Freya, showing us the safest route to hop across an oozing, spongey stretch. 'Now stick to the path.' And we follow the hoof prints and wheel ruts along the raised track, all the way to the Mosses' cottage.

Fergus Moss meets us at the door. He is dressed in a strange green robe and is wearing a pair of antlers on his head. 'Don't laugh,' he warns us.

Dolly and Deedee snort behind their grubby little hands.

'I think you look wonderful, Fergus,' Freya says firmly.

'Mammer is making sure the robe isn't too long.

She doesn't want me to trip over in front of everyone. And she wants you to try on your dress too, Freya.'

Fergus and Freya are to be the Green Man and the Earth Spirit at the ceremony of Springtide Fires this Sunday. Freya hasn't stopped talking about it for weeks – it's even worse than when she was Queen of the May.

'I'd *love* to try it on!' Freya squeaks, darting to the door.

But then Mister Moss appears at the threshold and blocks the way into the cottage. 'Aren't you forgettin' something, girls?' he twinkles.

'Oh!' I step forward. 'We pledge a lamb,' I say and put my hand out to Mister Moss.

'We pledge a *lamb*,' Freya says, elbowing me out of the way.

Mister Moss laughs and shakes both our hands. 'We Mosses promise four barrows of turf for the Fernsby fire.'

'Make it a good lamb, please, Willa!' calls Missus Moss's voice from somewhere inside the cottage. 'Not a stringy one.'

'A good fat one!' I call back in reply.

Mister Moss smiles and moves to one side and we all troop in, ducking under Fergus's antlers.

Missus Moss is carrying a shimmering green gown all embroidered with purple flowers. She holds it up against Freya. 'Oh, you'll look fine in it, Freya,' she says. 'I'll just nip it in a bit at the waist. And we'll put green ribbons and sweet violets in your hair. What do you say?'

Freya nods. 'Yes please, Missus Moss.' She has a regal smile on her face and Fergus is gazing at her like an adoring pup. Freya takes a length of green ribbon from the table and tries it against a lock of her gold hair.

'Ooh, Freya!' Dolly sighs, and Deedee reaches out to touch the dress. 'So pretty!'

'What do you think, Willa?' Freya asks, tipping up her chin and flouncing a bit.

'I think, standing side by side like that, you and Fergus look a bit like a hedgerow, and you'll want to watch out for sparrows nesting in your skirts.'

'Ha! You're just jealous.'

'I am not.' And it's true. I'd rather die than be the Earth Spirit and have to dally about the Springtide Fires with a boy, throwing flowers at people. I was so relieved when the elders chose Freya instead of me, and Fergus as her Green Man. There was some grumbling in the village about a peat-bogger getting such an important job, but Grammy spoke up for him and she won in the end – she usually does. Freya is over the moon, and the Mosses are so proud.

'You know,' Missus Moss says as she tacks up the hem of Fergus's robe, 'most young 'uns who play the Earth Spirit and Green Man together end up wed a few years later.'

Fergus goes red.

'Arms out! Breathe in!'

He puts his arms out and goes even redder.

'You look like a scarecrow, Fergus!' sniggers Dolly, and Deedee sniggers too. 'An old beetroot-face scarecrow!'

Mister Moss winks at his son. 'Don't you worry, lad,' he says gently. 'You'll be the envy of the whole village come Sunday.'

Then Darcy pipes up. She has been watching Freya swaying and preening with the green dress held up against her. 'I remember Grace in that dress,' she says softly, and everyone goes quiet.

'Aye.' Missus Moss smiles. 'Was it two springs ago? I think it must have been. And young Joss Cooper as her Green Man. We all thought they'd make a good match, but then, of course, Mister Kirby . . .' She stands up, takes the dress from Freya and hangs it from a hook on the whitewashed wall. 'Such dancing that year!'

'Any news of Grace?' Mister Moss asks.

We all shake our heads.

'She's safe,' I find myself saying. 'I know she is.'

'She's run off to be a dancer,' Freya blurts out. 'With the Full Moon Fayre.' And we all look daggers at her.

We know this must be where Grace has gone. I can still see my sister's face when Viktor told her they needed a new dancer – *A way out! A way to escape!* But none of us has breathed a word to anyone.

Freya meets our fierce looks with daggers of her own. '*What?*' she demands, crossly. 'The Mosses are our friends. They won't tell Dadder, or Silas Kirby.'

'Course we won't.' Fergus scowls from beneath his antlers.

'Anyway,' Freya goes on. 'Dadder must suspect Grace ran off with the fayre – they both vanished that same night – but he still can't find her, can he? No one knows where the Full Moon Fayre will turn up next. You can't track it down – it's impossible!'

'Nothing's impossible,' Darcy whispers, giving voice to my own thoughts, as she so often does.

I put my arm around her.

Mister Moss is looking at us. His kind face is a bit more serious than usual. 'Funny you should say that,' he says. 'Can you girls keep a secret?'

IO

'Keeping a secret is what Fernsby girls do best, Mister Moss,' Deedee says, and Dolly nods solemnly.

'Apart from Freya,' I mutter. I get a swift punch on the arm for that.

Mister Moss smiles. 'Come and look at this then . . .'

He reaches into an alcove high above the fireplace, and takes out a thin roll of parchment. He places it on the kitchen table and unspools it, smoothing it out. He puts stone cups and a doorstop at the edges to hold it flat.

'It's beautiful,' Freya says, touching the faded colours, the lines and shapes. 'What is it? A painting?'

'It's a map,' I say. And now I know why Mister Moss asked us if we could keep a secret. As far as folks round here are concerned, maps are almost as bad as books. It's the same thing as writing – putting something down on paper to make it knowable. Maps make you think about where you are, and where you *aren't*. They make you powerful. They put ideas in your head. Mister Moss would be in for the ducking stool if anyone knew he had a map of the Lost Marsh. And there's *words* on it too . . .

'How does it work?'

'You have to use your imagination a bit,' Mister Moss whispers. 'Imagine you are a bird . . .'

'A skylark?' Darcy asks quietly.

'Aye, little one. A skylark if you will – high up over the Lost Marsh, and you look down at the world below you . . .' His peat-stained fingers trace the shapes that quilt the map: the blue sea at the bottom, then the light-green fields of the farmed salt marsh. Here is the rise of a hill and a dark green forest; here, the brown turf of the peatbogs.

'Goodness,' breathes Freya, and Dolly and Deedee echo her: '*Goodness!*' We have never seen the Lost Marsh like this before – the vastness of it made visible, all at once.

'Look,' I say. 'These bits must be the mire.' I point at the black shapes snaking all through the Lost Marsh, and all around the edge of it too. The mire is unmappable, really – the deadly sucking mud shifts its edges with each changing season. But there are parts of it that always seem to remain, no matter how dry the weather or how gentle the tides. I read out the names from the map: 'Hollow Mire, Sorrow Mire, Rotten Mire, Forgotten Mire, Fishy Mire, Fox Mire and Flax Mire . . .'

'Goodness!' Dolly says again. 'I never knew the Lost Marsh was so big!'

Dotted amongst the greens and browns are the grey shapes of houses.

'This is Hollow-in-the-Marsh,' Darcy says.

'And what's this?' I ask, pointing at the shape of a tower.

'It's an old fortress – that's in a village called Foul-field – it's a day or so's ride from here. Just a ruin now, stuck in the middle of a sheep field. Odd place, Foulfield . . .'

'But how could a map tell you where the Full Moon Fayre will be, Mister Moss?'

'Well, it can't – not on its own. But a rag-and-bone-picker came by last week. Nice fella, he was – been all over the marsh, and beyond . . .'

'Beyond?'

'Aye – *far* beyond.'

I look at the map, and try to imagine the places that might lie beyond the outermost mire – places like in Grammy's books: cities and jungles, deserts and mountains . . . Were these the sorts of places that Grace might get to see, travelling with the fayre?

'This rag-picker said he'd hitched a lift with the Full Moon Fayre after it left Hollow-in-the-Marsh. Said they'd stopped at Foulfield, Dengemarsh and Hogback Hill, and were on their way to Frightwood when he caught a ride back down this way on a hawker's wagon.' He points at each village on the map as he says its name.

'I don't see how any of this helps,' Freya says. 'We need to know which village the fayre will be going to next, not where it's already been.'

'Look,' Darcy says, taking Freya's green ribbon from her hand and stretching it out across the map. The ribbon traces a straight line from Hollow-in-the-Marsh, through the other villages, heading straight towards the edge of the map where the doorstop holds it flat.

'It's going east,' Mister Moss says.

'What does east mean?' asks Freya.

Mister Moss moves his finger on the map. 'Going along this way, with the sea always on the right,' he says.

'East means *towards the doorstop*,' Deedee says, knowledgeably.

'So, the next village will probably be . . .' I study the map closely, extending the ribbon a little further. 'Gallows End – on the other side of Sorrow Mire.'

I look at the twisting black mass of Sorrow Mire, then I look back at all the villages scattered between here and there, trying to guess at the fayre's route.

'So, right now, Grace must be about here?' I say quietly, and I touch a spot on the ribbon near Frightwood.

'I'd say so,' Mister Moss agrees.

It is something magical – like looking into a crystal ball and seeing a vision of someone you know to be far, far away. 'Hello, Grace,' I whisper. And the green ribbon blurs against the colours of the map as my eyes fill with tears.

That night I dream I am a bird – flying high up above the marshes, looking down at the cut-out patterns of the fields and farms below. I know the Full Moon Fayre is down there somewhere in the puzzle of shapes, but I don't know where. And then I see her – my sister Grace – with white-feather swan wings, soaring and gliding across the tear-stained map, far below me. I try to call out to her, but she can't hear me. She beats her long white wings. She is frightened, fleeing, flying faster than I ever could – and she is gone.

II

The bride wears a long, pale gown, and primroses have been woven into the braids of her shining brown hair. Daisy Smith is the blacksmith's daughter, and she is marrying Pete Kirby – Silas Kirby's nephew. It is an arranged match – blacksmiths marrying saddlers – but it is a happy one: Daisy and Pete have been sweethearts for as long as anyone can remember.

There should have been two couples getting wed, of course – Grace was meant to marry Silas today – but no one is mentioning that. The wedding that isn't happening hangs above us like a rain cloud, and we are all trying to pretend it isn't there.

Somehow, Grammy persuaded Dadder to come along to the Springtide Fires. It would have been odd for him not to be here, with Freya being part of the ceremony and all, but we were still surprised when he agreed. He made us wait for ages — brushing his new coat, shining his boots, faffling in the farmyard with jobs that could have waited till later. We heard him cursing at the chickens as he rushed them into the henhouse and slammed the door shut behind their feathery bums. But eventually he was ready.

I look at him standing beside us now — smart and sober — dressed up like a gentleman in his coat and riding boots. What if someone mentions Grace? Or Flint — the horse that isn't really his? I hope he will be dignified in front of Silas Kirby and the elders. And I hope with all my heart that he is able to say something nice to Freya about being the Earth Spirit.

It is evening. The moon is rising over the village, waxing like a ripening peach. Handbells are chiming now, very softly — sweet notes ringing with the sunset all around the village green. And Daisy walks between the fires towards her groom. When she reaches him, Elder Warren uses a stick to draw a circle about their feet. He says the sacred words and they repeat them together. Pete takes Daisy's hand, and Elder Warren binds them together with a length of fine white cloth. They will keep this cloth to swaddle their first-born child.

They turn to face us all, smiling — and we are all smiling too. They are so happy, it would be hard not to smile. But then I see an unsmiling face in the crowd, and my insides curdle. Silas Kirby. His eyes and mouth are slack with grog, and he is looking this way: *Where's my bride, Nate Fernsby?* they say.

Someone starts playing a fiddle, and the bride and groom begin to dance together between the fires. Soon drums are banging and pipes are piping and everyone is clapping and jigging and swinging around. Slices of fruitcake and cups of honey wine are handed around by Grammy and some of the other elders. The triplets are holding hands, skipping together in a ring-of-roses.

'Come and dance with me, Willa?' A boy is standing in front of me. It is Joss Cooper – the lad who was Grace's Green Man two years ago.

'Dance?'

His freckled face smiles winningly: 'Aye – *dance* with me, Willa!'

'No, thank 'ee, Joss. I'm quite happy watching.'

He shrugs and grins and dives back into the jig.

Grammy is at my shoulder. 'Don't feel like dancing, Willa?'

'Not today.' I am watching the groom twirl his new bride around and around – faster and faster; I am watching the triplets spinning in a ring; I am watching Silas Kirby stagger his way through the revels, glaring at Dadder as he gets closer and closer . . .

Then someone else is talking. 'So, our Joss in't good

enough to dance with you, eh, Willa Fernsby?' It is old Missus Cooper – Joss's grammy. 'Not good enough to marry Grace, and now he's not even good enough for a jig. You Fernsby girls have a mighty high opinion of yourselves if you think a Cooper is beneath you.'

'Willa's not in the mood for a jig, Missus Cooper,' Grammy says. 'Let her be.'

But Missus Cooper is like a puffed-up old hen, and once she starts pecking, she won't stop.

'He's a good lad, and strong. Not as handsome as his brothers, but he's cheerly and jokesy, our Joss. Any girl would be proud to dance with him. What's the matter with him, Willa? Not *clever* enough for you?'

The word 'clever' is an accusation. I look straight into her beady eyes. I just want her to go away. I feel anger bubbling up inside. I feel that I am about to say something cruel . . .

But then Grammy puts her hand on my arm and answers on my behalf: 'Your Joss is a lovely lad, Missus Cooper. I'm sure Nate meant no slight when he betrothed Grace to Silas.'

Missus Cooper's face puckers with rage. 'No slight, indeed! We're the laughing stock of the whole village. You say it was Nate's decision, but I say it was *you*. It's always you – ever since we were lasses – always buzzin' about the village like a queen bee – stickin' your oar in. Meddlin'. No respect for tradition and the way things ought to be. There's whispers in the village that there's *books* in that house of yours. And folk want to know why you've got a field full of fat lambs when they lost so many. They're sayin' you put the evil eye—'

'Oh, hush now, Missus Cooper,' Grammy says. 'Come, now, you know that's nonsense. Just because our farm is on higher ground, out of the marsh—'

But Missus Cooper is shaking her head. 'There'll be a reckoning for you,' she mutters. 'You and your *cleverness* – just you wait . . .' And she bustles away into the gathered crowd.

I am breathing fast, ready to fight. *The evil eye? Are folks really saying that about my grammy?*

'Don't worry, Willa,' Grammy says, giving my shoulders a gentle squeeze. 'She's full of hot air, that one – always has been. Had it in for me ever since I marrid your late grampy. He was *her* Green Man, you see – many moons ago . . .'

But then something happens. The music has changed. Grammy's voice fades with the dying of the fiddle. She turns, along with everybody else, towards the fires.

It is just the drum now – a heavy, steady beat like the heart of a giant – and the dancers are all still. They part, as if furrowed by a plough – boys to one side, girls to the other. The sun has set and darkness has stolen upon us swiftly. The flames flicker and crackle, hot and high. And then two figures appear – two black shapes with the bright fires towering behind them.

They walk, as if from the flames themselves – a boy with a crown of antlers, a girl garlanded with flowers. The beat is primal, drumming in our chests and our blood. The dark figures walk slowly towards us. They scatter blossom on the earth and on the bowed heads of the bride and groom, who kneel before them. A blessing.

I know it is just Fergus and Freya. I know it is a ritual – a show of shadows just like the one I saw with Grace at the Full Moon Fayre: a sort of magic woven with darkness and light. But there is an ancient, unearthly power in this moment, all the same – the fires, the drumming, the Green Man and the Earth Spirit. I remember Grace as the Earth Spirit – I remember her dancing like the fire itself, whipped into bright shapes by the night wind. I can almost see her . . .

The figures walk towards us slowly. And it is Freya's face that emerges from the shadows, of course, not Grace's. She is painted with swirling patterns of peat-ink, her eyelids blackened with ash – and I shiver in spite of myself. She is beautiful. A huntress, a queen.

There is a shuffling and stumbling beside me, and Silas Kirby has reached us at last. He stops and turns to see what everyone else is looking at. My sister Freya.

'Tha's one of your lasses, in't it, Fernsby?' Silas slurs.

'Ar. Tis,' says Dadder. And he actually looks proud. He smiles at Silas. Perhaps this is a moment of parley –

a truce. They will work something out about the horse, the debt . . .

Silas's eyes narrow. 'Tell you what, Fernsby,' he says. He swigs from his bottle of grog and licks his lips.

I have a horrible moment of premonition. I know exactly what he is going to say.

He grins at Dadder and gestures towards Freya.

'I'll have that one instead.'

12

Dadder's head is in his hands. He sits, slumped over the kitchen table, tugging at his hair with rigid fingers.

'Not Freya, Dadder,' I say, my voice trembling. 'You *can't* give him Freya – she's not old enough to be wed yet—'

'Will you shut *up*, Willa!' Dadder explodes, sitting up suddenly. His eyes are red as furnace coals. 'Let me *think*, the lot of you! Go away and let me *think*.'

But my boots are planted on the floor and my arms are folded across my pounding chest. Angry heat is prickling its way up my neck, and I will not budge. 'Give Flint back,' I say. 'Just give the horse back and Silas will have no power over us.'

Dadder looks at me as if I'm mad. As if he'd rather

set the farmhouse on fire, with all of us in it, than lose that magnificent horse – the one thing that makes him feel proud . . .

'Give – him – Flint?' he says. His eyes are narrow, his voice is dangerous.

Grammy is watching him from her chair. The triplets are sitting on the floor around her skirts. Freya is standing with her back to the fire, still in her Earth Spirit costume, her face tear-streaked with ash. She was a goddess less than an hour ago. Now she is smudged and faded.

'I won't wed Silas,' she sobs, trying to keep her chin high. 'I won't! I'll run away, like Grace!'

'Don't mention that girl's name in this house,' Dadder growls. 'She made me look a *fool*—'

'You *are* a fool!' I snap back. '*You* drove Grace away, and now you'll drive Freya away too. Is that what you want? For *all* of us to—'

BANG – he pounds the table with his fists. 'Yes! That's what I want – that's exactly what I want – to be rid of the lot of you. *Six* girls – *six*! A man never suffered such hell as this—'

'Stop it,' Grammy says. Her voice is low and brisk – the same voice she uses with the chickens when they get too pecky.

'*You* keep out of this,' Dadder snarls, wheeling round to face her. 'This is none of your business. They are *my* girls and they will do what I *damn* well tell them to do! If I tell Freya to wed Silas Kirby, then that is what Freya—'

'But you're forgetting the curse, Dadder.' The voice comes from somewhere near the fire. It is small, but clear as the bells on the village green.

Darcy.

Her big dark eyes are open wide, and there is no hint of a tremor in her voice – no fear at all.

Dadder garps and blinks. His face twitches – he is outraged that she has spoken to him; she is a rat biting at his foot. 'Did you . . . say something?'

But Darcy is undaunted. She stands up to speak to him. Instinctively, the rest of us stand up too. Grammy's hand is on Darcy's shoulder as if its touch can protect her. 'The curse says Freya can't get wed, Dadder. The second daughter has to stay at home, or . . .'

'Go on,' Dadder growls. 'Go on, Darcy. Say it. Freya has to stay at home, and Willa has to work on the farm, and Dolly and Deedee have to get wed, *or*?'

She says it simply: 'Or the sixth daughter will bury you. Stone dead.'

A beat. My chest is thudding like the drum at the fires. Dadder scrapes his chair back and moves towards Darcy. He is breathing heavily, his nostrils flaring like a bull's. 'And is that what you are going to do?' He whispers, 'You horrid little demon, you *curse* upon this house . . .'

We are all holding our breath. I move silently across the flagstones – am I close enough to grab Dadder's arm if he raises it?

He crouches so that his face is level with hers. 'Are you going to bury me stone dead, Darcy?'

Our whole world splits in two when Darcy says, 'Only if I have to, Dadder.'

Dadder stares at her. We all stare at her. Dadder laughs at the ridiculousness of this threat, but then his face darkens and his lip curls. He lifts his hand—

'NO!' I scream – I think perhaps all of us scream it at once – and something blasts through the air – all fiery like sparks. Dadder flies back into his chair with such force it crashes to the floor and splinters beneath him.

I don't know what just happened. My common sense blinks and tells me it must have been the fire crackling and popping – Dadder must have lost his balance and staggered backwards . . . We are all looking around, confused, apart from Dadder. He is looking straight at Grammy, and the fear on his face says *sorcery*.

He picks himself up, his eyes still fixed on Grammy. His hands are shaking. '*Witch*,' he breathes.

'Dadder,' I say. 'Don't be stupid – it wasn't a spell – just sparks from the fire – there's no such thing—'

'I've had *enough*,' he splutters madly, and he points a shaking finger at me. 'You get out. Get out of my sight. You answer me back, you call me *stupid* and a *fool* – and I won't *stand* for it any longer. Get out – you can sleep in the stable, for all I care. I won't have you under my roof a moment longer.'

'It's Grammy's roof,' I snarl back. 'It's not your house, it's *Grammy's!*'

'OUT!' he bellows, and the force of it propels me towards the door.

He turns to Freya next: '*You* stop your snivelling, and if your wretched sister doesn't come back by next spring, you'll have to wed Silas Kirby instead.'

'But, Dadder – Fergus—'

'But *Fergus* nothing,' he sneers. 'As if I'd let you marry a filthy peat-bogger anyway. And if the pair of you try to run away, I will HUNT YOU DOWN!'

Freya runs up the stairs, sobbing.

Dadder points at Darcy. 'And you. If you *ever* threaten me again, I will do what I should've done all those years ago – wring your skinny neck and throw you down the damn well.'

Darcy doesn't flinch, but Grammy puts an arm across her. 'And what about me, Nate?' she says in a level voice.

I see that fear flash in his eyes once more. 'You had better bite your tongue, woman, and never use your *powers* on me again, or I'll tell all the village what you are. And who will look after your precious little chickens if you're nothin' but ash and bone?'

Dolly and Deedee whimper, and Grammy gathers them closer.

'It's all right,' I find myself saying. 'He doesn't mean it – he'd never—'

He spins around, furious. 'I mean every *damn* word. Why are you still here? I said LEAVE! Out with the animals, where you belong!' He yanks the door open and I am blinded by the blackness of the night. He shoves me hard down the steps and I feel that I am falling into a bottomless pit; I collapse in a heap in the cold mud of the yard. He towers over me like an ogre: 'You're a cuckoo in the nest, Willa Fernsby. I knew it when I first saw you, and your mammer did too. A *cuckoo* daughter, since the day you were born.'

And he slams the door.

I sit there in the mud, fuming. I want to charge back into the kitchen and yell in Dadder's face. *You BULLY, you PIG,* I want to scream. *You're the one who should be living outside with the animals!* But I don't. Something has changed in him – snapped suddenly like an old rope pulled too tight. He is broken and dangerous and more frightening than I've ever known him before. He has chucked me out of that door more times than I can remember, but it has never felt quite like this.

I head into the stable and find a clean corner to curl up in. Jet ignores me, but Flint watches curiously as I make myself a nest in the straw. Even as I am doing it, I can feel my fury growing rather than fading. *He expects me to live out here with the animals. He wants me to stay on* the farm and keep doing my jobs, but he won't have me in the house. He needs me to stay, because of the curse . . . And that's when I decide. I won't stay. I won't live with the animals. I won't be a slave to the curse, or to him. I won't be druv.

I'm going to run away too.

13

'Watch out, Willa,' Darcy hisses. She is leaning out of our bedroom window, dangling a big bundle wrapped up in my bedsheet. Dolly and Deedee are giggling behind her. 'Don't drop it on her head!' Dolly shrieks.

I step back, and the bundle falls into the yard with a *THWUMP*.

'Thank you!' I call back.

But the window shuts before we can say goodbye, and I can hear a muffled voice – low and growling. *Dadder*. Did he hear us talking? Does he know the triplets have packed my things for me? I strain my ears, listening for raised voices or the crash of furniture, but it is all quiet again. I creep back into the fuggy dark of the ~~~~~~~~~~ Dadder to guess that I am running away. I want it to be a horrid shock. I want him to be sorry that he threw me out, sorry that his precious curse is in tatters, sorry that he said what he said . . .

A cuckoo daughter. What did he mean by that, anyway? Just that I am a child he never loved? And what did he mean he knew it when he first saw me? And that Mammer saw it too?

A cruel claw hooks into my heart.

Did he mean that Mammer hated me too?

I sit down heavily in the straw, the bundle in my hands.

I've always felt different from the others, but I've never known why or how. The triplets have each other, and their games that no one else understands. Grace, Freya and I have always been the Big Ones, but the truth is that I've always felt like the ugly duckling, tagging along behind my taller, fairer sisters. I'm stuck in the middle, all by myself. I'm the loud one. The one that starts the fights. I can hardly think of a day that's passed without Grammy saying, 'Always lookin' for trouble, you are, Willa.' She's right – I am always looking for trouble. At least, I'm always looking for something. And maybe now, setting out on my own, I'll find it at last.

Soon I'll be far, far away from Dadder, putting miles of marshland between us. I try to push his spiteful words out of my head, pack them away into a heavy box and force the lid shut . . .

Then I open up the bundle the triplets dropped out of the window. What have they packed for me? I just have to hope Darcy was in charge; if it was Dolly or Deedee, there'll be nothing but a string of beads, a straw hat and a rag doll . . . I pull out the awful horse-hair blanket first – scratchy, but at least it will keep me warm. Then some clothes – the blue cloak that once belonged to Mammer, and a pair of old riding breeches (Grace's perhaps? I can only think they are for warmth too). There is a hunk of cheese, a lump of bread, and a big slice of honey cake, all wrapped up in a cloth to keep them fresh. Goodness knows how they got those without Dadder noticing. *It must have been Grammy*, I think. Someone has also thought to pack a tinderbox. It's a pretty metal tin – very old, as it's been repaired with solder across the lid – and inside it there's a flint, a steel and some charcloth, for starting fires. There is also a soft bag that clinks when I pick it up. I peer inside and a dozen gleaming coins wink back at me. Next, my hand closes on a square, heavy object, and I draw it out. *Tales of the Marshes* – the book of folktales Darcy borrowed from Grammy that cold winter's night just before Grace ran away. It makes me smile that my littlest sister thinks something to read is just as impor-tant for my survival as food and warmth, or perhaps she put it in there because it is one of Mammer's books and she wanted me to keep it . . .

Suddenly it feels like a proper goodbye. Maybe for ever. I swallow and try not to cry. I am going to have to be stronger than this if I'm going to survive on the marsh all alone.

I pack up the bundle again, my heart whumping away. *I am leaving home. I am leaving Hollow-in-the-Marsh. I might never come back . . .*

The horses are restless. Old Jet munches and mills about. He lies down to snooze for a few minutes, snoring like a saw. Then he scrapes his hooves on the floor and farts loudly as he struggles to get up again.

Flint dozes standing up. He keeps watch over the farmyard, poking his noble head over the stable door to have a good look whenever a rat scratches over the cobbles, or a barn owl screeches.

I try to gather my thoughts, but I am in such a state it is like herding panicked sheep. *Come on, Willa, you need to make a plan.*

If I can't be at home with Grammy, Freya and the triplets, there is only one place I want to be, and that is with Grace.

I will track down the Full Moon Fayre and find her. Perhaps I will join the fayre too. They might give me a job looking after the animals. I feel like a character in one of Grammy's stories – setting off into the bigness of the world with just a bundle of clothes and a handful of coins. *I could die*, I think. *I could die out there on my own – sucked down into the mire, starved to death by the wayside, beaten by robbers, gored by wild boar.* I need to be clever about this – I can't just wander off across the Lost Marsh and hope I'll bump into the Full Moon Fayre. I need . . .

I sit up suddenly. I know exactly what I need.

There is somewhere I must go before I leave Hollow-in-the-Marsh.

I get myself ready, putting on Mammer's warm cloak and packing my blanket back into the bundle. I eat a piece of bread, pat the horses goodbye, and sneak out into the farmyard. Flint whinnies softly, nuzzling my back as I leave. It is the first time he has done anything like that. I turn and look at him. He nods gently, pushing his grey nose into the crook of my arm. After months of us cold-shouldering each other, he has decided to trust me at last.

I am amazed at how quickly all the hatred and resentment melts away.

'None of this is your fault any more than it's Grace's, is it boy?' I whisper.

He lets me stroke his nose and cheek, and I say goodbye again. I find myself giving him all my other goodbyes too – goodbyes that are really for Grammy, Freya, Dolly, Deedee and Darcy. Tears well up in my eyes as I put my arms around the horse's neck and feel the warmth and the strength of him.

And then I have an idea so wonderful it stops

my tears at once.

I could take Flint with me.

I could steal Dadder's horse!

I can't help but smile a wicked smile when I think about how crushed he will be . . .

'What do you think, Flint?' I whisper. 'Do you want to come with me and find Grace? I could do with your help.' *And I would feel safer too*, I think. *I wouldn't feel so alone.*

But what if Dadder is so angry he takes it out on the others?

The bridle is already in my hands, paused in mid-air. Flint watches me with his dark, shining eyes, and I am reminded of Darcy – her fearlessness – that clever, fierce fire that burns within her. Darcy wouldn't want me to be worried. She may be tiny, but she is stronger than I am, and she has Grammy to look after her. If I ride Flint, I can find Grace much more quickly . . . And then, quite suddenly, I have to stop myself from laughing out loud: I remember the riding breeches packed into the bundle for me.

'Thank you, Darcy,' I whisper.

I look up at the shadow of the house. It is so dark I don't know if the small shape I can see at our bedroom window is my littlest sister, or just a spectre conjured by the starlight and my own wishful heart. I picture Darcy's face, her serious little salute: *Go, Willa!*

I salute back.

Flint dips his head so I can put his bridle on. I buckle it up clumsily, my fingers trembling a little with cold and the shock of what I am about to do. I lift the big saddle on to his back. He stands perfectly still as I tighten the girth strap. Then my hand finds a mark on his haunch – a criss-crossing of thin wounds, raised and inflamed. Welts from Dadder's riding crop.

Any last doubts I had about stealing Flint are blown away like straws in the wind. 'You're coming with me, you beautiful boy,' I whisper. 'We're going to find Grace, and we're going to look after each other. All right?'

He butts his nose gently against my shoulder and blows warm, horsey air out of his nostrils.

I think that means, *Yes*.

14

The riding breeches must have been Grace's or even Mammer's, as they are too big for me, but I'm used to wearing hand-me-downs. I've rolled the legs up and tightened them with a cord around my waist, and they are warm and comfortable. I am heading towards the Mosses' cottage – avoiding the main tracks in case Dadder wakes early, finds Flint gone, and sets out to find us. I follow the route we took on the day of the spring promises: skirting the green, where the ashes of last night's fires are still smouldering; past the windmill and Silas Kirby's farmhouse; over his big field, cutting across the common land and the bottom of Glorious Hill.

When I left the farm, the sky was still night-black and the dawn was just a grey whisper over the marsh, but the sun is rising now. It is going to be a beautiful spring morning – cool and dazzling with primrose-yellow light – the sort of morning that fills you up with brightness and makes you feel giddy as a lamb.

Riding Flint is nothing like plodding along on old Jet. It's more like being carried along on a great white wave, or a cloud driven by the wind. As we make our way through the lush grass at the bottom of Glorious Hill, I find I am able to shut away all my fears about the journey ahead as easily as I shut away the chickens at dusk. Spring is a time of beginnings, and here I am beginning an adventure with a heart made light by the sunrise and the wonder of this stolen horse.

There is a broad, flat stretch of path ahead, beside Grey Brothers' Pond at the bottom of the meadow. The turf is sweet here, and Flint's step is all dancing and springy. I offer an encouraging squeeze with my legs and he takes off – galloping within moments of being given his head. I have never flown like this on a horse before. And I know now that taking Flint was the right thing to do – possibly the best thing I have ever done – if only for this delicious moment of speed – joyful speed – and breathless freedom! 'WOOOOOO!' I shout. 'WOOOHOOOOOOOOOO!' And Flint stretches out, gathering up his legs even faster, thrumming across the ground like he has been waiting for this moment all his life too.

'Good boy,' I laugh as he slows up. 'Good boy, Flint.'

I find my seat and give him a pat. I think of what a handful he has been for Dadder, with all his bucking and prancing. 'Just a bit choosy, aren't you, boy?' I say. 'You know your own mind, don't you?' And he nods happily. Whatever happens now, we are friends, Flint and me.

The path narrows and curves around beneath the willows, and by the time we clop over the wooden bridge, Flint is walking calmly again. The horizon opens up in front of us — endless fields, some mud-brown, striped with corn shoots; some greener, but shimmering wet. On these salt-marsh meadows, sheep cluster together on raised mounds, waiting for the tide to turn. The ditches between the fields are brimful with water and, as the sun rises higher over the marsh-land, they gleam like ribbons of gold. A breeze rattles the reeds and grasses. The land is so flat here, the sky is almost everything. On a day like this, it's like being in a huge bubble of blue; but on a stormy day, the bigness of the sky makes you feel like a speck — at the mercy of the big black clouds that bulge above and all around.

We turn in to the sun and take the path towards the bogland. The ground is heavy and wet, each step releasing the stink of things that have been rotting for centuries. Freya makes this journey more often than I do, and she knows the safest shortcuts across the peat-bog. I try to steer Flint from one patch of higher, drier ground to another, but he ignores me completely, choosing his own sure-footed route, and after a while I give up tugging on the reins as he clearly knows better than I do.

I find myself checking over my shoulder more and more often. There is nowhere to hide here in the bogland – no trees at all, just flat, brown, squelching turf – and the brightness of the early morning suddenly makes me feel stupidly exposed. I want to be slinking along close to the ground, like a weasel – hugging the shelter of a hedgerow – but here I am perched on top of a big white horse: impossible to miss, even from a mile away. I keep hearing the splashing of footsteps, and I twist around expecting to see Dadder striding furiously towards us, but no one is there.

Everyone knows it's bad to be out on the marsh all alone – particularly on the bogland, or, worse, amidst the sucking mud of the mire. The eeriness of this place creeps under your skin, even by daylight.

A curlew flaps into the air and calls loudly – a sudden, mournful mew – and Flint and I both jump, spooked by the strangeness of the sound.

At last we join the main track and reach the Mosses' cottage. The shutters are still closed, but grey-blue smoke is curling from the chimney. I loop Flint's reins over a fence post and find him a bucket of fresh water to drink.

'Hello?' I call, tapping softly on the front door. 'Hello?'

Then bolts are drawn back, and the door creaks open. Mister Moss is standing there with a steaming mug in his hand and a worried frown on his face. 'Willa – you all right? Come in.'

I sit at their kitchen table, warming my feet by the turf fire and drinking a cup of hot milk. Fergus stumbles into the room, rubbing his eyes and looking annoyed that I am me and not Freya. I tell them what has happened. They were all there at the Springtide Fires last night – they saw Silas and heard what he demanded, but they don't know Dadder's decision: that Freya must marry Silas next year if Grace doesn't return.

Fergus goes a peculiar colour. 'I'll go and get her,' he says. 'Right now. Can she come and stay here, if she needs to?'

His dadder puts his arm around him. 'Don't worry, son. It's a long time until the next springtide weddings. But, yes, of course Freya's welcome to come here – if that's what she wants. We'll keep an eye on her, and see what Nate does next. You know what he's like, blowing hot and cold . . .'

Missus Moss is almost as upset as Freya was last night. 'How could he *say* such a thing?' she rants, clanking around the kitchen. 'Him and Silas Kirby are as bad as each other – bullies, both of 'em! Why don't *they* get marrid and keep their damn horse, and drink themselves into early graves and leave everyone else alone!'

'Aye,' I sigh. 'That would be for the best. But, about that damn horse . . .' And then I tell them the rest of it. That I am running away to join Grace at the Full Moon Fayre – and that I have stolen Flint.

Fergus opens the front door and squints at the brightness of the morning and the whiteness of the horse tethered to their fence. 'Oh Willa . . .' he says quietly. And all three Mosses look at me.

'I know,' I say, although I have not truly felt the weight of the theft until this guilt-heavy moment.

'He's not even Nate's horse to steal,' Missus Moss says. 'After you left the Springtide Fires last night, Elder Warren made a proclamation: since Grace wasn't there to be wed, your dadder has to return Flint to Silas Kirby within the month, or he'll be put in the stocks for theft.'

Theft.

'You've stolen a stolen horse, Willa,' Fergus says, and it is so awful that I want to laugh. The edge of Fergus's mouth twitches too, and then all four of us are laughing – quite helplessly, until tears are in our eyes. But the horror of it all is not lost on me. It won't just be Dadder trying to hunt me down now, it will be Silas Kirby too . . .

'You could take him back?' Mister Moss says. 'Or leave him here and I can do it for you – take him straight back to Silas?'

But I don't want Flint to go back to Dadder or Silas.

I think of the scar on the horse's neck, and the whip welts on his haunch. I shake my head. 'I'm looking after Flint now,' I say quietly.

'Then you need to go,' Mister Moss says, and his face is more serious than I've ever seen it before. 'And you can't come back until all this is sorted out somehow.'

'And will you keep an eye on Freya and the triplets? Please.'

They all nod. Fergus stands up straight, nearly as tall as his dadder. For a moment I see the ghost of antlers over his head. *Freya's Green Man.*

'Of course,' Mister Moss says. 'We'll do what we can for Freya and the others. You need to set off to find Grace now, while you've got a good head start.'

'Aye. I'll go.'

'You'll be needing this.' And Mister Moss reaches up to the alcove above the fireplace and pulls out the rolled-up map.

'Thank you,' I say. 'I was hoping you'd let me borrow it. I'll take good care of it, I promise.'

'It's the map's job to take care of you, Willa,' he says. 'To help you find Grace quickly and safely. And you'll need this too.'

He reaches further into the hidey-hole and pulls out a little leather-bound box. He flips it open. Inside is a small, round instrument of some kind, made of polished brass. The lid pops up to reveal a white face and a hand that spins around.

I've seen something like it before, attached by a chain to Elder Warren's coat. 'A pockety-watch?'

'Not a pockety-watch,' Mister Moss says. 'A compass.'

'You won't always have a doorstop to tell you which way is east —' he smiles — 'but this little needle will know where north is, and then . . .'

He shows me what to do. I watch, entranced, as the metal pointer flickers back and forth, finding its way. Then he lays it on the map.

'It's magic,' I breathe.

'A sort of magic, aye,' Mister Moss agrees. 'Lots of things are magic, aren't they? Things in nature, things in the sky, clever things like this. Strikes me magic is a way to explain things we don't understand. Some folks see the wonder of it, but other folks will be afeard. Keep it safe. Keep it hidden.'

'I will.'

They follow me out to say goodbye.

'Don't lose your way, Willa,' Missus Moss says, giving me a hug.

'I won't,' I say, waving the map at her before tucking it safely into the lining of my blue cloak.

'I don't just mean on the marsh,' she says. She puts her hand on her heart. 'Don't lose your way in here either.' And she kisses the top of my head. 'Or in here.'

15

A marsh harrier is circling above us – its dark feather fingers and thumbs splayed against the brightness of the sky. It screams – a chilling sound that thrills across the nothingness.

Flint and I have been travelling all morning – squelching through the boggy turf, north, then east, across the endless salt marsh. There are men here, digging out new ditches to protect the grazing land from surging seawater. They wade about, knee-deep in the brackish slime. They tip their hats to me, and I nod back.

For a moment, I think about heading south towards the sea – I've never actually seen it properly. In Hollow-in-the-Marsh, the sea is simply an enemy – an invader threatening our land and our livestock with each turn of the tide – but I know Grace never felt like that. She loved the seaweedy smell of it that drifts over the marsh when the wind is just right. She used to dream of swimming in the cold waves like a seal . . . Suddenly, I realize that Grace has always dreamt of *freedom*. Perhaps the Curse of Six Daughters was worse for her. At least it gave me and Freya things to do. I've always liked to think that I'm a good sheep farmer *in spite* of the curse rather than because of it, but who knows how it has shaped us all, deep down. Would Freya still bake the best kidney pie in Hollow-in-the-Marsh if the curse hadn't made her spend so much time in the kitchen? And Grace? Grace has grown up waiting to be married off to the highest bidder.

No wonder she dreamt of freedom.

I look towards the sea one last time, and say farewell to the fresh salty sniff of it, then I turn east again. Grace is this way. And I need to move quickly.

Every now and then, when no one is near, we stop and I check the compass; I hold it steady in my flat hand and wait for the spinning, swinging needle to tell me which way to go. When we are far enough beyond the fields of Hollow-in-the-Marsh, we follow the compass needle obediently down a narrow bridleway. I do not know these tracks, these unfamiliar farms and cottages.

I keep my head down when folk trundle by on their carts – in case Dadder, following our trail like a wolf, asks people if they've seen us. I just wish Flint wasn't so eye-catching; people can't help smiling at him, and each time they do he lifts his neck and prances a bit.

As we head further across the Lost Marsh, I am aware of an anxious tugging in my chest, a cord pulling tighter and tighter the further I go from home. I have always thought of myself as a bold spirit, but now I am not so sure. The only adventures I have had before have been in my own imagination – playing in the fields or reading Grammy's books. It seems my soul is more tightly bound to home than I thought. And I am worrying about the animals too – my new lambs, even the silly old chickens . . .

'Grace is this way,' I say, out loud this time, and I nudge Flint into a purposeful trot. 'Onwards, Flint!' But it doesn't stop the strangeness of it all and the longing for home. I don't know what we'll find as we go into the heart of the Lost Marsh: it is a journey into darkness.

The sun is setting when we arrive at a crossroads. Bulrushes grow tall all around us. There is no wind here, not even a breath. I stop, confused, and look carefully at the map. Flint stamps impatiently.

I get out the compass, let the tiny needle spin and settle, then I check the map again. Something is wrong. We should be approaching Hogback Hill by now, but this ground is low – I can tell by the sludgy mud of the track . . .

At last, I find where we must be on the map – a place called Foulfield. Mister Moss told us about this village, the one with the old fortress, but I should be much further east by now . . . I have taken a wrong turn, following that uncanny little arrow north, when I should have set it on the map first and then found the road heading east.

I sigh.

Not the best start, but we have veered only slightly off course, wasting time on this winding bridleway. It could have been worse. We could have ended up in one of the two mires that cradle Foulfield like cupped hands – Rotten Mire and Forgotten Mire.

The first stars are dotting the darkling sky over Foulfield. The ruined fortress is here, in the middle of a sheep field, just a little way off the track – as Mister Moss said. It is sad and beautiful and strange. Its empty windows are full of sky. The full moon is rising beyond it – large and round. It is an odd colour tonight – tinged with red and gold, like a copper coin. *A blood moon.* I feel a little shiver of superstition. I don't want to be out here all alone, I want to be at home by the fire, with the others, and Grammy too, knitting in her chair . . . Then I hear her voice in my head: *Superstitions do us harm. They bind us with fear.*

I won't let fear take hold of me now. It's just the moon, that's all. I need to think about Grace, and catching up with the fayre. According to that rag-picker fellow, the fayre stopped here in Foulfield after Hollow-in-the-Marsh, then it went east to Denge-marsh and Hogback Hill . . . This full moon means it will be moving on tonight, leaving the village of Frightwood, if that's where it still is, and then, perhaps, continuing east towards Sorrow Mire and Gallows End. If I manage not to get lost again, Flint and I should be able to catch up with it within a few days.

'Walk on, Flint,' I whisper, and we head into the village. We will have to stay here for the night now, and, after spending much of last night on the stable floor, my bones are aching for a proper bed.

Children are playing in the lane up ahead. I stop to fill my flask with water from the village pump. 'Do you know a place I can stay?' I ask the children.

Three grubby faces garp back at me.

'Is there an inn?'

'Come here!' Their mammer rushes across the lane to gather up her chicks. 'Come in now – quickly!'

'Good evening, missus,' I say to her. 'Do you know a place I can stay?'

She stares at me, then bundles her three little ones back to the cottage across the lane.

'I – I was just wondering if there was a place . . .'

But they have vanished into the cottage and the door slams behind them.

I am struck by the sudden silence in the village. No

shouting or singing from an alehouse, no dogs barking . . . I heave myself back up into the saddle again; the creak of the leather and the clop of Flint's hooves on the lane sound unnaturally loud.

As we pass a row of cottages, shutters close with a bang. I hear keys clicking in locks, bolts grating. A face flickers at a window.

'Something odd here, Flint,' I murmur, and he whinnies softly in reply. The blood moon is rising higher now. Shadows melt together in the growing darkness.

We reach the alehouse – The Plough. It can't be much past supper time, but the doors are closed and the windows shuttered. I try to ignore the goosebumping of my skin, the nervy shaking inside me. *What is going on?*

Then there is a light footstep on the lane behind us; Flint wheels around, alarmed, as a lady hurries past.

'Sorry,' I say, 'do you know – is there somewhere I can stay?'

'Haven't you seen the moon?' she says. She points upwards, but her eyes are looking at the ground, wide with fear. Her hand is a visor, shielding her gaze from the sky.

'The moon?'

'Aye – the moon. The *blood moon*, child! You need to get home!'

'I don't understand . . .'

'It's terrible bad luck to look upon the blood moon,

or for it to see you – *terrible* bad luck! Everyone knows that.'

'Do they?'

'Aye. Sickness, or madness – or worse!' She is at her front door now. She shoos us away. 'Hurry, child! Hurry home!'

'I *can't* go home . . .'

But she has gone. Flint and I are alone once more.

'What'll we do, Flint? Where shall we go?'

He turns around and clatters back down the lane, breaking into a twitchy trot as the darkness thickens and the collywobbles get the better of us both. He is heading towards the ruined fortress.

'Good idea, boy,' I say. The sound of my own voice helps to keep the creeping shadows at bay. 'It's better than no shelter at all.'

The fortress may be a ruin, but there is still something about being within the outline of its fallen walls that is reassuring. I take off Flint's saddle and bridle and let him munch the thick tufts of grass that are growing between the cracked stones. Eventually, he wanders into the field itself. 'Don't go too far, Flint,' I call. He stops and looks back, then starts grazing alongside the sheep as if he were one of them – a great, leggy sheep amidst the small, pillowy ones. This wasn't what I had planned for the night, and the creepiness of Foulfield village has spooked me to my marrow, but I feel better now we have found a place to make a camp.

First things first. A hawthorn tree is growing up through the cobbles of the old gateway, and I scrabble around beneath it, collecting prickly sticks and dry leaves. I pile them up in the most sheltered corner of the ruin, take out the tinderbox the triplets packed for me, my thumb stroking the vein of solder that holds the old box together like a silvery scar. I strike sparks into a fragment of charcloth. A tiny flame catches at last and I feed it with twigs and leaves until it is dancing and happy. I coax it, blowing very gently, and then, all of a sudden, it flares into a proper little fire, and I heap up the sticks and broken branches until it makes a good, strong blaze which purrs and crackles.

Magic, I think. A flint-struck spark always feels a little magical to me. The birth of a flame. I think about bread rising in the oven; milk churning into butter; swifts flying back from faraway lands to find last year's nest in the eaves of our house. Then I think about Mister Moss's map and compass, Grammy's gold-leafed books hidden away in the darkness of her cupboard – how some things are just so magical that folks are afeard of them . . .

I look up at the moon.

In Hollow-in-the-Marsh, a blood moon might make folks coo and shiver. Some might bring their sheep in for the night, light fires or scratch shapes on the chimney breast to keep the demons at bay. But here in

Foulfield, the superstition is bone-deep. Fear quakes the air like the beating of wings.

I won't let it in.

'You're not an evil omen,' I whisper to the moon. It is as round and perfect as the paper lanterns at the Full Moon Fayre. My mind goes back to that evening – the smoke and dazzle of the magic show; the dancers flying like birds over the main arena; the shadow-puppet show I saw with Grace – sunset over the dreaming marshland, the murmuration of starlings in the rose-blush sky . . . That was magic too, of course, but a different kind – the clever sort of magic that would fall away to nothing at the drawing back of a curtain.

I add more sticks to the fire. I unpack my bundle, and use the scratchy blanket and Mammer's cloak to make a bed against the fortress wall. The earth is damp and spongey, but the old stones must have soaked up the day's spring sunshine – they feel warm to touch. I eat the last of the bread, along with a mouthful of cheese and a fuzzy old apple Missus Moss gave me as I was leaving. I reach to the bottom of the bundle, looking for another warm layer of clothing, but instead my hand closes on *Tales of the Marshes*.

The firelight makes the gold-leaf lettering on the cover all twisty and shivery. The book falls open at the story I read to the triplets – 'The Marsh King'. My heart gives a little lurch of fear, and I turn the pages quickly. The last thing I need when I'm camping out in a spooky ruin is a fairy tale about an evil sprite who had built his own castle somewhere in this marsh . . . I look around and shudder. *An evil sprite who may or may not still haunt the mire, preying upon lost souls . . .* It might be fun if the others were here. I think of Darcy reading the story aloud in her low, serious voice; Deedee pulling a googly-eyed face to make Dolly squeal; Freya shushing them as she lies on her back and gazes up at the stars . . .

But not on my own. Not beneath a blood moon.

I take a steadying breath and focus on the shapes of the letters instead of the words themselves – letters drawn by my mammer's hand. I turn the pages, and imagine her fingertips curling each corner. At the end of the book, there is something I've never noticed before – a missing page: a raw, torn edge where a whole leaf has been ripped out. The page before it bears the title for the final tale in the book: 'The Story that Never Was'. And then – nothing. No tale at all. I frown, confused, wondering what Mammer was thinking of when she made that little mystery for us.

Mammer.

Grammy.

Home.

The fire flickers, making the world beyond it seem all the blacker. The sky is frighteningly big above me – pitch-black and cloudless. It will be a cold night. The blood moon is rising higher now, and the words of that lady in the village make me almost afraid to look at its ghostly shape.

Could it be bad luck?

I try to laugh at the idea, but the laughter dies like a feeble flame in the night air. Anything is possible on a night like this – madness and magic, ghosts and demons and evil sprites; the darkness swarms with them all. *Grace ran away on the night of the winter moon*, I think . . . I can feel superstitions starting to crawl beneath my skin again, and I shake myself.

I look around for Flint. He has wandered back within the ruin now and is grazing on the grass and meadow flowers here. The firelight shimmers across his white flanks. Bats emerge from the ruined tower, swooping down one by one and flittering into the dark. Flint watches them. I know he will keep an eye out while I sleep – if I *can* sleep. All sorts of dark, hateful fears are stalking through my mind now – the sort of thoughts that usually wait until the wakeful hours of the night . . . *A cuckoo in the nest. A cuckoo daughter* . . . Is it possible that Mammer despised me, just as Dadder does? Or did he just say that to hurt me?

I huddle down into my nest and try to shut out the thoughts by shutting my eyes tight. But I can't get comfy; I can't get warm; I can't get used to the empty space above and around me – no low-beamed ceiling, no beds crammed up beside mine, no sisters snoring just inches from my face. I have only been away from the farmhouse for a day, but I miss it horribly – the fug of the peat fire, the smell of damp, soapy washing, the stew bubbling in the heavy-bottomed pan: the warm stench of home.

16

It is a cold, terrible night – oddly silent, oddly still. Flint paces the ruins like a guardsman, watchful and jumpy. I sleep in snatched moments, plunging suddenly into dark dreams that I immediately try to scramble back out of, only to find the fire dying and my cold-sweating back pressed against the stones of the fallen fort. Marsh bugs buzz in my ears. I have never been so glad to see the dawn.

Flint and I set off at first light, and we are both glad to put Foulfield far behind us. 'We'll ride straight on to Hogback Hill, Flint,' I say, checking the compass and map at the crossroads and taking the track that leads east.

Skeins of geese flap overhead as we ride, heading home after wintering on the salt marsh. Their honking and cluthering is cheerful; I never thought I would miss Dolly and Deedee's brainless noise this much. A breeze blows, brisker as the hours of the morning go by; the sunlight is warm. 'A good laundry day,' Grammy will be saying as she bustles about the farmhouse, flinging windows open and gathering up all the bedsheets, nighties, skirts and undies she can carry. I smile, and I ache at the same time.

There is a market at Hogback Hill, and the track to the village grows busier the closer we get. The noise and the bustle of it all feels like a balm after the raw loneliness of my journey. But when we arrive, the whole marketplace is cloaked in smoke – grey and choking. There are fires lit all around the edge of the square – not like the big Springtide bonfires back home, but braziers burning awful hot. The air is thick with the reek of green wood and wild garlic.

I fill my water flask from the village pump in the square while Flint slurps at the trough. We both drink deeply, then I muddle my way through the smoke and the people, leading Flint by his reins. He is not used to such busy, noisy places and I don't think he likes the smoke either. I have to hold his head firmly to stop him from skittering about.

I make my way to a baker's stall and buy a pie and a loaf of bread. I put the coins in a boy's big red hand.

'Has the Full Moon Fayre been this way?' I ask him,

blinking through the smoke. I need to know if I'm on the right track. I wish I could follow Grace's trail like a sheepdog follows the scent of a lost sheep — nose to the ground, through puddles and nettles and bramble-thick ditches, closer, closer . . . But I can't. Questions will just have to do.

'Aye,' he says, handing me back some copper coins. 'Couple of months back.'

I feel a little glow of hope. 'Do you know where it was headed next?'

'Frightwood, I think.' He turns to serve another customer.

'Thank you.' I smile. *I am doing well. I am heading the right way. I will find Grace soon.*

The sound of low singing rises up through the hubbub and I turn to see a string of people following a cart around the edge of the square. The voices get louder and I recognize the words of the chant: '*To the earth, to the earth, to the earth that fed you; to the arms of the earth that gave you life . . .*'

It's a funeral.

'Marsh fever,' the baker's boy says, nodding towards the procession. 'Watch out. It's everywhere at the moment.'

Marsh fever? We don't often get it in our village, but on warm evenings, you can sometimes see the swarms of bitey-flies hazing the air over the bogland and Hollow Mire. They say, if you get bitten, there's a good chance you'll sicken with marsh fever. Old folks like Grammy call it 'Smuggler's Fever' or 'Lovers' Death', as it's only smugglers and lovers who are out on the marsh late on a summer's night.

'Is that why you've got the fires lit?' I smother a cough.

'Aye – burnin' herbs keeps the bitey-flies away.'

I watch the funeral procession as it turns the corner and disappears.

To the earth, to the earth, to the earth . . . I remember hearing those words for the first time, clutching Grammy's skirts as she juggled two of the tiny squirming triplets. Sobbing and sobbing for my mammer, and nine-year-old Grace hoisting me up into a hug so warm it made me feel safe in spite of everything. *My big sister* . . .

I *will* find the Full Moon Fayre. I *will* find Grace – but my head is pounding with tiredness and my throat is burning with the smoke. I need to rest and get my strength back, or I'll be fit for nothing.

I spy an inn on the quiet side of the square. A man in an apron is sweeping the step outside the front door.

'Afternoon,' I say. 'D'you have a room for the night?'

'Aye,' the man says. 'And stable for this fine fellow?' He nods at Flint.

'Please.'

The man leans his broom against the whitewashed

wall and leads us around the back of the inn to a row of stables. Flint rolls in the clean straw the moment I take the saddle off him, then he leaps back up, dances about like a foal, and tucks into a big bag of hay.

The innkeeper smiles. 'Handsome colt, that,' he says. 'Don't s'pose you want to sell him, do you? I'm in the market for a good horse.'

'Sorry,' I say. 'He's not really mine to sell . . .'

'Ah – stolen, eh?' the man jokes.

'Ha!' I laugh, but it rings out false in the dusty air of the stable. For the hundredth time since I left home, I wish Flint weren't quite so eye-catching, and I pray that we are not being hunted down across the Lost Marsh . . .

There is a high-pitched buzzing in my ear. I flinch, slapping at the side of my head. I itch at my hair.

'What's that?' the man asks. He goes all pale. 'Bitey-fly?'

'Just a gnat, I think.'

'There's bitey-flies swarming up from Sorrow Mire,' the innkeeper says. He looks suspiciously at the air around me, then quickly leads me back to the front of the inn. 'Just be safe inside before sunset, and keep your window closed. Don't want to catch marsh fever, do you?'

I think about last night, sleeping out in the open in the ruined fortress . . . I scratch at my head again. I hope the blood moon wasn't bad luck after all.

I look up at the sign that swings outside the inn – a laughing demon wearing a crown of bones.

The innkeeper sees me looking. 'Welcome to the King's Head, miss!' he says, holding the door open for me.

'The King's Head?' I go inside.

'Aye. You'll have heard the old fairy tale, I suppose? The Marsh King?'

I nod slowly, staring at him. *But I didn't know other people knew it – I thought it was just my mammer's story . . .*

'Well, the tale round here goes that one midsummer, the Marsh King captured a thousand swifts and swallows – snatched their little birdy souls right out of the air. And ever since then we've had plagues of bitey-flies. Not so many birds to eat 'em up, you see?'

The innkeeper laughs again. 'Marsh King, indeed! Folks love old tales like that, don't they?'

I nod and smile, trying to forget the cold tremor that ran through me when I saw that demon with his bone-crown – as if he had somehow crawled out of the pages of Mammer's book . . .

17

The room is dark and chilly, despite the warmth of the afternoon, but it seems clean enough. And a bed, however hard, has got to be better than a cold stable floor, or the flagstones of a ruined castle. But just one bed in this big room . . . It looks so lonely, so odd, not like our crammed-in cattle stalls back home. There will be two empty beds in that room now . . . Just four sisters left.

When Grace left so suddenly, I remember it felt like the whole world was suddenly empty and big and strange, and everything felt wrong. It's not like grieving for someone who's died, because when someone just vanishes like that, you know – you hope – that they are still alive somewhere. So it's just an endless, wishful ache. I wonder if Grammy and my sisters feel the same about me, now I've gone. I wonder if Dadder is sorry he ever said those horrible things.

I light a fire to drive the dampness from the room, and the innkeeper brings hot water. I eat the pie I bought at the market, have a good wash and climb into bed. It is only early evening, but I am so overwhelmed by the comfort of pillows and blankets, so deeply exhausted after two sleepless nights and two days in the saddle, that I cannot stop my eyes from closing . . .

I sleep deeply through the darkness, until the dawn light seeps, all pale and bright, through the thin curtain. My head still aches, and there is a shivering deep in my bones. I roll over, pull the blankets up to my chin, and doze again. This time my dream is haunted by chanting voices that swoop through my mind like owls through a forest: *To the earth, to the earth, to the earth.* There is a fire, a Springtide Fire . . . Flames are ribboning the sunrise sky . . .

I wake up, coughing. There is a smell of smoke in the room.

I climb out of bed and go straight to the window that looks out over the market square. The braziers are still smouldering. They must have been burning all night. The dawn breeze is scattering ashes over the cobbles, and the smoke is drifting up against the walls of the buildings. It reminds me of the blue smoke from the Mosses' cottage – their fire burns all through the year, to keep the damp out and the marsh bugs away.

Grammy burns herb-bundles on the fire too, sometimes, especially when we are sick – camomile, nettle and feverfew. I sniff again. I am thinking of home now, and home makes me think of Grace. I'm still terribly tired. My limbs ache and my head is pounding, but I mustn't lose any more time. I need to pack up my bundle and get Flint saddled. I need to catch up with the Full Moon Fayre.

Frightwood is the next village on the trail and, as far as I know, the last village the fayre stopped at. The landscape is different here – chalky slopes covered with trees rise up from the flat, festering marshland. It is another warm day, the skies bare-blue and empty. There are speckled butterflies in the hedgerows, insects humming in the air. Now and then a cloud drifts out of nowhere and we are scattered with raindrops, but they feel more like summer squalls than spring showers.

A beekeeper's cart overtakes me as the road widens. The woman driving the horse is wearing a long gauze veil to protect her from stings. *Odd that she should be wearing it when she's not handling the bees*, I think.

At the top of a rise, I stop to take in the view. There are orchards either side of the track – rows and rows of apple trees. But before me, the forest of Frightwood sweeps down to a vast expanse of dark grass and muddy marshland. It is as if we are standing on a mountain, rising up from a great, murky sea. *That's Sorrow Mire*, I think: the biggest mire in the whole of the Lost Marsh. The stink of it rises on the warm air — that brackish tang; that stagnant smell of things mouldering in the deadly ooze. And there, in the distance, is another rise crowned with trees. *That must be Gallows End.* I feel a bubbling rush of excitement and my tum goes all fluttery. 'I'm coming, Grace,' I whisper. 'I'll be there soon!'

'Not if you don't cover yourself up, you won't,' says a low voice right beside me, and I jump. There is a man resting his arms on a barred gate. He wears a gauze veil too, so his features are as blurred as the distant hills. *Another beekeeper?*

'Get yourself covered up, lass,' he says. 'Or you'll be bitten before the day is out. And then you won't be goin' anywhere.'

Of course. The veils aren't for beekeeping, they're to keep off the bitey-flies. I notice Flint flicking his tail in irritation, the presence of whining midges in the air that I have barely noticed until now. I brush my hands over myself to check none have landed on me. My skin feels all prickly and crawling.

'You all right, lass?' the man asks.

'I . . . I don't know.' Suddenly the pounding in my head has become almost unbearable. My skin feels hot. Burning hot. The colours of Frightwood are all swimming together into a dreamy greeny-blue . . . black at the edges now . . . I feel myself falling forwards, my arms closing suddenly around Flint's neck.

'Easy, there.' The man is helping me down. 'Let's get you inside, shall we, lass? Look like you need a bit of help. My sister'll look after you.'

I'm fighting against the blackness that keeps closing in on me. I'm aware of a footpath to a white cottage, my feet fumbling along beneath me. A young woman opens the front door.

'Got a poorly lass here, Sarah,' the man says.

I collapse into a chair.

'Have you bin bitten?' the woman asks, bringing me a cup of cold water.

'I don't know,' I manage to say. 'I don't feel very well . . .' I take a sip of cold water.

She is looking at me closely. Examining my face, my forehead.

My hand goes to the place she is looking at, and there is a lump beneath my fingers, hot and itching. My heart clenches with dread.

That night in Foulfield — sleeping out in the open . . .

'I'll be all right,' I murmur, thinking of Gallows End on the other side of the mire — *I'm so close now. I can't get sick — I'm nearly there.* 'I just need a bit of a rest, that's all.' But I know it's more than that. 'Not everyone dies from marsh fever, do they?'

'Not everyone,' she says kindly. Too kindly. 'What's your name?'

'Willa,' I whisper.

'I'm going to treat the bite with a hot poultice, Willa. It'll smart a bit.'

My chest is vibrating. The veins in my neck and scalp are pulsing painfully. The poultice is so hot I cry out, but the young woman holds it tight against my head. She is so straightforward that I trust her completely.

'You hold it,' she says, placing my hand over the wad of cloth. 'I'll check you for more bites. Press it on as hard as you can bear it.'

So I do. I clamp my teeth together and press the scalding hot pad on to the tender bite. *I can't get sick now*, I say to myself. *I can't get sick now – I haven't got time . . .*

I hear a whinnying from outside. 'Flint,' I murmur. 'My horse . . .'

'Don't worry,' the man says, heading back towards the door. 'I'll put him in the stable for now. He'll be safe.'

'Thank you . . . What if he's bin bitten too?'

'Bitey-flies can't get through horse hide,' Sarah says. 'It's just us that get sick – and the odd piggywig too. Always bad this time of year, bitey-flies. Did you see 'em? Those black clouds over Sorrow Mire?' She has found another bite on top of my head, where my hair parts down the middle. 'Brace yourself, lass.'

Fresh hot poultice on raw, swelling bite . . .

My head and neck are burning, pounding with hot,

infected blood. Tears are coursing down my cheeks but I don't know if it is from the pain or just because I am so scared and so far from home and I want my grammy.

The woman is still talking – about the bitey-flies, the mire – but her voice is fainter with each moment. Time is slurring. I close my stinging eyes and rest my head on my arm – pulsing, pounding . . .

I can feel her placing a fresh, scorching-hot poultice over the bite on my forehead, but I hardly flinch. An ice-cold shuddering has started in my gut. My skin is all goosebumps despite the burning heat.

I hear the clack of the door latch, footsteps on the flagstones, and the drawing in of breath. The words of the man and woman sound as if they are from far, far away – whispering through a cloud of heat and buzzing insects . . .

'She don't look good.'

'Poor lass . . .'

18

I am not dead, but I am not quite alive.

The first hours of pain and fever are the worst, then it settles into a rhythmic burning and shaking with cold, and a dreadful aching in my head and my bones that goes on and on, as days blur into nights. Most of the time I am in a deep, deep sleep, but sometimes I manage to pull myself up to the surface, like hauling a heavy bucket up from a well. I peer out through hurting eyes at the too-bright room. I sip water or broth from a cup held to my lips, I try to say something, but then the deathly aching drags me back down again, and there's no use fighting it.

Time passes, and I don't die. Somehow, very slowly, I get stronger. The brother and sister are still looking after me in their cottage by the apple orchard. They are called Amos and Sarah Starley, and this was their dadder's farm. Sarah makes wonderful broth and she has a laugh like a happy magpie. Amos is more serious than his sister. He is good with horses, and he knows everything there is to know about apples and orchards and cider and such. They have the same eyes – big and grey, and a bit sad when they are not smiling.

They have been looking after Flint for me. He is safely stabled with a fat pony called Pippin. My bundle of things is beside my bed. When the cottage is quiet at night, I read *Tales of the Marshes*. I dream about marsh mermaids, bog monsters, and the Marsh King himself. The more I read the stories, the more real they become. I wonder about Mammer's mysterious 'Story that Never Was', and that steals into my dreams too. Sometimes it is a great adventure, with dragons and mountains; sometimes it is the tale of six sisters who lived happily ever after on a sheep farm with their grammy.

When the fever was at its worst, it was Grammy's face I saw looking down at me. It was her cool hand on my brow.

The window of my small whitewashed room is open full, to let in as much air as possible, but a gauze is nailed tightly across the frame to stop bitey-flies coming in. Sarah tells me I have been ill for more than three weeks. She says the plague of bitey-flies has passed now. As the season bloomed into late spring, the winds changed, bringing clean air from the sea, and birds came from the countryside all around to feast upon the bitey-flies – swifts, swallows, house martins, gorging themselves on the thick black swarms and feeding up the fluffy chicks in their nests.

'You're still too weakly, Willa,' Sarah insists, propping me up and feeding me some vegetable soup. 'You can't possibly travel to Gallows End all alone.' Her face is puckered with worry. 'And even when you're strong enough, you mustn't cut across Sorrow Mire.' Her voice goes quiet and tight: 'That's how our dadder died. Not long before you came. He was going fishing early one morning, heading for the carp pond near Gallows End, and he took the shortcut across the mire. We never saw him again.' She is waiting for me to look her in the eye. 'You mustn't even think about it, Willa.'

'I'm so sorry about your dadder,' I say. 'But you mustn't worry about me. I'll take the long road around the mire – I promise – and Flint will look after me.'

She smiles, unconvinced. 'You're still not strong enough.'

'I'll be fine. I just . . . I can't wait any longer.'

The fayre is at Gallows End right now. We heard the music drifting across Sorrow Mire last night, saw coloured lanterns jewelling the hillside.

'The moon is nearly full,' I say, 'and then the fayre will be gone again, and I might never find it. I might never find Grace . . .'

There is no road east beyond Gallows End; this is where the green ribbon ends – we have nearly reached the doorstop. Beyond it lies the looping tail of Sorrow Mire, and then – to the east and to the south, there is nothing but sea. The fayre will have only two choices: to turn back into the Lost Marsh again, or to head north: over a toll bridge, through the ancient forest and across the chalky downs to the world beyond.

I must catch the fayre at Gallows End.

'You'll be strong enough to make the journey soon,' Sarah says. 'And you'll find the fayre and find your sister. Don't worry. You just need to wait a little longer.' And she touches another spoonful of soup to my lips.

I am watching the moon rise from my window: an almost-full shape in the starless sky. I am sitting on a chair for the first time since I collapsed in the kitchen downstairs. I am sick of lying down; my twitching limbs feel restless. I nibble the corner of a bread roll Sarah left for me, and sip a beaker of milk. 'Eat as much as you can manage,' she said, but my appetite has still not come back. My tum feels empty but weak; it does not want to be bothered with proper food yet.

I rummage through my bundle, looking for *Tales of*

the Marshes. Something else flies out with it, clinking on to the floor. I pick it up. My heart gives a happy, hefty thump. It is a brooch – Mammer's brooch – a shining black stone set in silverwork. I remember when the triplets first unearthed it from a box of treasures under Grammy's bed. 'Look!' Dolly cried, holding it up for us all to see. 'It's a omlet!'

'You mean *amulet*,' Freya laughed. 'You mean a lucky thing they have in fairy tales to keep them safe.'

'I do mean exactly that,' Dolly said. 'A omlet.'

'Omelettes are made of eggs, you daft duck,' Grace said, ruffling her little sister's curls.

'It's a *magical* omlet,' said Darcy. 'Look! You can *see* the magic in it. All shiny . . .'

It stuck like goosegrass: from that day Mammer's brooch had always been our magical omlet. And it had been on many a daring quest with the triplets. It had even smashed a perfect round hole in the kitchen window during one particularly fierce battle between an elf and two frightful trolls.

I smile, gripping the brooch in my hand. I know how much it means to the triplets. It was kind of them to give it to me for this quest of my own.

The road outside is quiet. A tawny owl *keewik*s a few times, and there is an answering *hoohooo* from the horse-chestnut trees beyond the orchard. I smile, thinking of my chestnut trees at the top of Glorious Hill. Then I press my face to the gauze and squint at the tiny lights of the Full Moon Fayre over at Gallows End. I listen for the distant wisps of music, but instead I hear sounds coming from the other direction.

Voices, and the clip-clop of horses' hooves.

It's awful late for folk to be out riding . . .

'There's an inn at the bottom of this hill,' says a man's voice. 'The Gate. We'll stop there for supper. If the moon's bright enough, we'll keep on for Gallows End tonight. Awright?'

'Ar,' comes the weary reply. And a cold shudder goes right through me.

Dadder? It can't be! Has the fever returned? Am I mad? Perhaps this is just another nightmare and I am still asleep . . .

But then I can see them – two men on horseback – and even from this distance, even through the gauze and the dull haze of moonlight, I know it is Dadder and Silas Kirby. I shrink back a little, though I know they cannot see me up here in the darkness. My heart hammers against my ribs and I feel clammy, sweaty.

Thank goodness Flint is in the stable behind the cottage, not grazing out in the paddock. Almost as if he can hear me thinking about him, he whickers and stamps.

Quiet, Flint. Stay quiet!

Silas's grey mare has stopped. 'Trot on, Silver,' Silas hisses, kicking her hard. But she doesn't move. She is looking this way.

Of course! Silver is Flint's *mother*. And now Dadder's horse has turned this way too. Jet can hear his old stablemate . . . Poor Jet – coming all this way from the farm, when he's on his last legs already. Dadder is cruel for bringing him. I can see how tired he is – the droop of his head, the heaving of his ribs. Even if he makes it to Gallows End, he'll never make it home again.

Silver whinnies softly, still looking this way.

I can't risk them hearing Flint's reply. Quickly, I untack the top corner of gauze and hurl my bread roll out of the window so that it sails over their heads and lands with a whoosh in the hedgerow beyond them. A pheasant explodes into the air, flapping noisily and coughing its shrill, urgent call. Poor Jet jumps, jerking his head so hard he nearly throws Dadder off, and Silver dances on her hind legs before spooking into a sideways canter and making off down the hill, with Silas cursing and clinging on tight.

'Middlin' good work, Willa,' I murmur to myself. I watch Dadder try to stay in the saddle as Jet trips and skids down the hill after Silver.

After the relief comes the horror: what if they find Grace before I do? They will drag her home to be wed. I have to get to the Full Moon Fayre before them – and warn her that they are coming . . . As I sit there in the quiet moonlight, a plan shuffles together in my mind. I might still be weakly, but if I want to save my sister from being married off to Silas Kirby against her will, I have to go now.

I find my clothes, all washed and folded for me (I have been wearing Sarah's old nightgowns for the past few weeks). I get dressed and put on Mammer's blue cloak, fastening it at the neck with the omlet brooch. I heave my bundle up on to my back, then I tiptoe down the stairs. I have to move slowly, with one hand steadying me against the cool stone wall. I step into the kitchen. It feels very odd to be up and moving about in the room where the fever first took hold of me. It all looks different in the dark. My knees are wibbling, so I sit down for a minute to get my strength.

I can't do this yet, I think.

But I have no choice. I have to warn Grace they are coming.

I pack some food into my bundle, and fill my water flask from a jug standing by the window. I place a pile of shining coins on the table – to pay for the food I have taken, and to thank them for looking after me through the fever.

19

Flint is so pleased to see me. He nods and swishes his tail up; he can't wait to get out of the stable. And he seems to know exactly where we are going. As soon as I drag myself up into the saddle, he sets off towards Frightwood village and the inn Silas mentioned. With any luck, they'll be resting the horses now and eating a good, long supper.

It is cool and clear. Over Mammer's cloak, I am wearing one of the Starleys' long beekeeper veils to keep any last bitey-flies at bay. As we pass the glowing windows of The Gate, I pull up the hood of the cloak and urge Flint into a busy trot.

Soon we are clear of Frightwood, and I have that buzzing, breathless feeling that I am winning a race – stretching out my lead with each mile we cover. I feel a

bit stronger now, more normal – the fresh air is helping, I think. Flint slows to a walk, and I knot the reins,
lifting the veil a little to eat one of Sarah's bread rolls,
and wash it down with a few gulps of water. Even
chewing is tiring, my jaw aching after just a few
mouthfuls. *If old Jet can make it all this way*, I say to
myself, *then I can manage this last stretch.*

The lane here is flanked with trees – huge and
ancient. This is the forest of Frightwood. Branches
reach into each other over my head to make a tunnel.
In the moonlight everything seems eerie and haunted –
it turns the branches above into glowing white bones,
as if we are inside the ribcage of a monstrous skeleton.
An owl sweeps silently over us. Flint's ears flatten and
he jitters about, eyeing the darkness on either side as if
it is crawling with wolves.

I wonder if he was hoping to have found Silver and
Jet by now – he must have heard them when they
passed the cottage. Or perhaps he recognized Silas and
Dadder's voices and is frightened they will hurt him
again.

'It's all right, boy,' I say. 'It's all right. We'll be with
Grace soon. You remember Grace, don't you? You
liked her.'

I talk about Grace. How she was the best dancer in
the village, and the best singer too. How she made the
sweetest, lightest honey cake. How she always knew
just how long a hug needed to be, so you always felt

better and never too-much squeezed. How she could make your nightmares go away by singing Mammer's old lullaby: *A damsel slept beside a brook, a-dreamin' and a-dreamin'* . . .

The song seems to soothe him a little, and his ears come back up. 'Good boy,' I murmur as we emerge from the tree tunnel at last. 'Brave boy.'

It is almost dawn by the time we reach Sorrow Mire. The darkness is beginning to wane now, but a thick white fog swirls over the lowland before us. The path forks here: left, to stay on the main track that skirts the edge of the mire, or straight on to cut across the middle of it. I turn Flint left. But then I stop. There is a noise on the road behind us: clopping hooves, low voices. Just distant echoes, dulled by the thick, damp air of the mire. I can only hear the tone of the voices, not their words, but I know by the tightening of my gut that it is Dadder and Silas. They can only have stopped briefly at the inn if they are so close behind us.

I can't let them catch up with me. I can't let them find Grace before I do . . .

Suddenly I am turning Flint around, abandoning the safe, winding track to the left, and sliding down the muddy path that leads straight out on to the mire.

They'll be sure to take the longer, safer path. This way, we'll beat them to Gallows End . . .

My heart is beating all shuddery and fast. The fog is

thicker than I thought.

'Just a bit o' mizzle, Flint,' I murmur. 'It'll clear as the sun rises.' Flint seems unsure. He stops, and tries to turn back. He whinnies nervously. 'Hush, boy,' I whisper, praying Silas and Dadder didn't hear him. 'It's all right. This way.' And I pull him back around.

We set off once more. The ground is sodden: slurping, sucking.

I am trying not to think about my promise to Sarah, or about her dadder, who disappeared crossing Sorrow Mire. I am ignoring the words of Mammer in my head: *Beware the dangers of the marsh, my darlings. Beware the mire* . . . I am shutting out the voices of all the elders back home: *Never set foot on the mire in the dark, children . . . Never cross the mire alone . . . Never, ever set out in the fog . . .*

We have been told time and time again about the many ways in which the mire will try to kill us. Sometimes the truth, and sometimes fairy tales – all jumbled up together to scare us into being sensible.

Here on the reeking mire, with the strange fog wreathing around me, the fairy tales feel more real than ever before. The rolling coil of an eel in the mud becomes the tail of a bloodthirsty marsh mermaid. Even the smallest black puddle becomes the hidey-hole of a bog troll – deep enough to swallow up a horse, leaving no trace but a few thick-filmed bubbles popping on the surface . . .

I grip the damp reins. Flint is treading slowly and carefully. I reach down to pat him – firm and reassuring. The warmth of his neck somehow brings me back to my senses.

I stop and check Mister Moss's compass to be sure the track in front of us is taking us the right way. The fog is so thick now that I have to wipe water droplets from the glass before I can see how the needle is lying. 'I think this is right, Flint,' I murmur. 'We'll just keep to this path.'

But it is not as easy as it sounds. The murky light and the soupy fog mean that I can only see a very little way ahead, and the path keeps branching into other raised tracks, most of which are only bluffs that stop suddenly and then plunge down into ditches. There are places where the main track has flooded and the way forward is hidden under dark, peaty water. Here and there, folk have left old planks and boards for crossing deeper puddles, but they are treacherous and rotten, and Flint knows it. He lengthens his stride instead, or leaps from standing – like a great white hare – and I cling on tightly.

We stop every few minutes to check the compass and make sure we are still heading in the right direction, not just wandering in a hopeless circle. We are doing well, I think.

But then there is a man's voice behind me – so close it makes me gasp. One hand flies up to cover my mouth. My legs tighten around Flint and he lurches forward, startled.

'Shhh,' I whisper, slowing him back to a steady, squelching walk. I look around but I can't see anyone there in the fog. It was Dadder, though – I know it. *Why didn't they take the long way round the mire? Are they . . . following me? Do they know I'm here, just in front of them?*

I have to be very careful now. I can't talk to Flint out loud. I have to hope he doesn't whinny or huff too loudly. The skin on my back crawls with fear as the voices get even closer; my legs are twitching to urge Flint on, but I force myself to sit floppy as a rag doll. If I'm not very careful, Flint will feel how scared I am, and if he spooks here on Sorrow Mire, that'll be the end of us both. I fix my sights on the path ahead. *Slowly, slowly, keep to the right path, Willa . . .*

'Runned off with a boy, I thought,' says Dadder's voice, suddenly clear as a tolling bell.

Sound moves strangely through mist – they could still be a furlong behind, or they could be almost on top of us. *Thank goodness for this fog*, I think. It is the only thing keeping us hidden from them.

'I searched for *months* and found no sign of Grace – you know that, Silas. I did the best a man could. I'll warrant she's at the bottom of a ditch somewhere. Now why don't we go back to that nice inn and rest up the horses?'

'Because I *swear* I saw my horse pass by the inn

window, that's why, Fernsby.'

I bite my lip and curse silently. My veil and cloak might have disguised me, but there's no disguising Flint . . .

Silas's voice continues, booming, bullying: 'And if I was right, and I *did* see my horse, then that was your Willa riding him, and she'll lead us straight to Grace. We'll bag the whole damn lot of 'em at once, won't we!'

'I don't feel right, Silas,' Dadder says. 'Somethin's bitten me on my hand. I felt it bite me. It's all swelled up now . . .'

'Afraid of a little midge bite?'

'There were talk of marsh fever back there – you saw that man at the inn, din't you, all got up like a beekeep? What if I've got bit by a bitey-fly?'

'I don't care if you've got bit by a bitey-fly, Fernsby.' Silas's voice is cold and cruppish. 'I don't care if I have to drag your carcass all the way to Gallows End. This is your mess and you swore to the elders you'd track your lasses down and get my horse back, so track 'em down you shall.'

'But, why can't we just rest up a bit? And why do we have to go 'cross the mire? Here we are, risking life and limb . . .'

'I know what I saw, Fernsby. I saw my horse on the road at Frightwood, and I'm pretty sure I heard him heading out on to this stinking mire. So this is the way we're goin'. And, anyway, your other one — what's her name? The Earth Spirit?'

'Freya.'

'*Freya* said Grace ran off with the Full Moon Fayre, and Willa would've gone right along after her. And she told us the way to go — Hogback Hill, Frightwood, Gallows End . . . So that's where we're going. And you'll not leave my sight until we've found 'em.'

Suddenly, my blood is pounding cold through my body. *Freya? Freya told them where to find us?*

I feel a sickening twist in my stomach and something rises up in my throat: half-chewed bread. Betrayal.

Freya? How could she . . .?

'I don't feel right, I tell you, Silas . . .' Dadder's voice again. 'Silas? Where've you gone?'

'Dang ye, Fernsby — I'm here on the track. Where in 'eck are you?'

'I'm on the track too. I think.'

'Well, one of us has gone wrong, then . . . *Argh* — this is a dead end . . .' Silas is cursing now. His voice is further away — over to the right somewhere, while Dadder is still behind me. 'Shout, Fernsby — I'll head towards your voice.'

'*This* way,' Dadder calls. 'I'm over HERE.'

But something very strange is happening. The fog is eddying in circles, thicker than ever, and the voices are moving with it. One moment Silas is over to my right, then he's to my left. Dadder's voice is shifting too.

'Silas? SILAS!'

Then it goes strangely quiet, and I can't hear Dadder or Silas at all. There is an odd light ahead of me – a soft glimmer through the fog. Could it be the sunrise? Or a cottage on the far side of the mire? It is a faint pink lustre. A marsh-fire, perhaps – a will-o'-the-wisp. But – it looks like a flickering lantern.

The Marsh King's lantern, whispers my fever-fuddled brain. The mire swims before my eyes. There is a dull thudding in my temples, and my hands are shaking so hard I can barely grip the reins. I am thinking about all the people who must have died in this mire – lost and frightened, taking just one wrong step, and then sinking down, down, drowning in that cold, stinking slop . . .

The ghost-light bobs eerily through the marsh reeds – a lantern being carried on a chain. I find myself drawn towards it – *This way, yes* . . . But Flint pulls me back on to the track.

'Sorry, Flint,' I breathe. 'You're right – this is the right path . . .' And I check the compass to be sure. I'm afraid my numb fingers will fumble the precious instrument into the mire, so I put it away again quickly. I am breathing faster and faster, trying to ignore the eerie pink light now, trying to shut out the warm, calling pull of it, like a familiar voice, like home . . .

Flint yanks the reins back and I realize I was pulling him off the path again. He is pawing nervously now.

'Sorry, boy,' I whisper. 'Shh, now. Easy. We're nearly there.' But that is a lie. I have no idea how much further we have to go across this dreadful marsh. At least the strange, luring light seems to be fading now. *Perhaps the Marsh King's hunt is over . . .*

'Silas?' Dadder's voice comes again. Fainter now, but more frightened. 'Silas!'

There is no reply.

'SILAS?'

Dadder's fear is infectious. I listen hard; I look this way and that way, but there is no sign of Silas or his horse, and I can't see Dadder either – only pale twists of fog, writhing like worms.

Flint starts suddenly, rearing up from the narrow path and skittering about. I grip the front of the saddle to stay seated. 'What is it, boy? An eel?'

But when I look down into the black water at Flint's feet, my heart starts skittering too . . .

20

Faces. There are faces beneath the water. Corpses staring up at me with terrible blank eyes. An old man. A girl. A warrior with a paint-striped face . . . Animals too – I can see a fox, a buzzard. All lifeless, floating here beneath the surface of the swamp.

I can't understand what I am seeing. I have stopped breathing. The reins lie loose in my hands.

'It's just the fever,' I whisper to myself. 'You're imagining it, Willa.'

I squeeze my eyes shut and then open them again, but the faces are still there. Their skin is all withered up like winter apples; their faded hair billows in the water like ghostly halos.

It's the fever — it must be. A nightmare. A trick of mist

and marsh-light . . .

Flint jolts me from my frozen horror, pulling and pulling at my numb hands. I can see the whites of his eyes, his nostrils flaring with each breath. He squeals with fright and jerks his head up hard, leaping forward into a canter to get away from the horrible dead-eyed things floating around his feet. I hold on tight.

Dadder is calling behind me – he must have heard Flint: 'Who's that up ahead? Silas – is that you?'

Old Jet whinnies to Flint, shrill and frantic, and Flint turns sharply, prancing on the spot – torn between getting away from the corpses and turning back for his friend.

I urge him on, muttering as loud as I dare: 'Come on, boy. Go on, now. Don't worry – Jet's coming too. Keep going, Flint. Good boy, walk on . . .'

Dadder again – his voice is failing, desperate: 'Who's that? I can hear you . . . Who is it? Willa? Is that you? Help me!'

I've managed to urge Flint into a trot – quick and jumpy – splashing through marsh-water puddles, and I can hear the sounds of Jet and Dadder behind us – sloshing, panting, groaning.

I am trying not to hear Dadder's cries for help, trying not to look at the corpses that I know are there, hanging in the murky water. But even with my eyes fixed ahead, I see flashes of colour beneath the water – the white beard of an elder; long red hair that surges in the water like seaweed, framing the face of a bride. *The victims of the mire – the poor souls who lost their way . . .*

'It's all right, Flint,' I breathe. 'Keep on, boy. Not far to go now.' I have no idea where these steadying words are coming from.

At last the path seems to be rising slightly – the mire seems shallower, the grass drier, greener. 'We're nearly there!'

The fog is thinning – the path rises further, widening to a proper track.

Thank goodness.

I feel Flint's gait relax at last – steady on solid ground.

Sorrow Mire is behind us. But so, of course, is Dadder.

I hear his voice again, fading into the mist now: 'Willa? Is that you? Help me, Willa . . .'

I am torn between pressing on and turning back . . . *Perhaps*, a hard little voice inside me says, *perhaps it is a fitting end for a man who has caused such misery – to die alone in Sorrow Mire.*

I dismount, tethering Flint to the branch of a twisted tree. I turn to stare back into the murk. And as I turn, I hear the map rustle in the lining of my cloak. *Don't lose your way.* My hand drifts up to my trembling heart, just as Missus Moss's did. *Don't lose your way in here . . .*

I walk back into the fog. I can just see the dark shape

of poor Jet, staggering, twisting, knee-deep in water. Dadder is a hulk, half-collapsed on to the horse's shoulders. He is yanking Jet's reins, pulling him the wrong way, deeper into the mire.

Can Dadder see the ghost-light too? Can he see the drowned faces?

'This way,' I call. 'This way!'

Jet turns immediately, ignoring Dadder's panicked kicking and flailing. I wade into the black water towards them. It clutches at my ankles, cold as death – like icy hands gripping and pulling me down. 'Come on, Jet – you can do it. This way, boy.'

The old horse's legs are shaking beneath him, his knees close to buckling. When he is close enough, I take the reins, prising them from Dadder's rigid hands and lifting them over Jet's head. I lead him slowly, carefully, one wet step at a time, and at last we are up on the track.

That hard little voice inside me that wanted Dadder to die alone in the mire is angry, confused. *You were supposed to be running away from him, not saving his life . . .* But Dadder is weak with marsh fever – woozy, barely conscious. He's no danger to me like this. I couldn't have just abandoned him. Jet is breathing loudly; he nudges my shoulder. 'And I couldn't have abandoned you either, boy,' I say out loud.

When we reach Flint, I untether him and the two horses greet each other, nose to nose, nickering softly.

There is a little grove ahead, just off the path – a few trees, a patch of grass, wild flowers. Flint lunges towards a clear stream that trickles through the grove, down to the sodden mire below us. The horses must be tired, thirsty. I take Flint's bridle and saddle off. He drinks noisily from the stream. Then he lies down to roll and stretch on the grass. It is as if he wants to rub Sorrow Mire from his coat, to scrub away everything that just happened. I pat his clammy flanks. 'Good boy, Flint – good boy. Brave boy.'

He snorts.

I yank Dadder down from Jet's saddle, on to the grass. He is unconscious now, and I can feel the heat of the marsh fever burning through his damp clothes. I manage to drag him a few feet, away from the track, towards the trees. Then I take Jet's saddle off and lead him gently to the stream. He drinks a little, then collapses, his sides heaving. Flint nuzzles him, blowing softly through his nostrils.

There is nothing I can do for our tired old farm horse. I just have to hope that a good rest will be enough for now.

I make a fire close to where Dadder is lying. I cover him with the scratchy horsehair blanket and he murmurs something, but I can't make out what he is saying. I watch him for a while: sweating, shivering, whimpering. I have never seen Dadder like this. Help-less. I should feel nothing but hatred after everything he has done: driving Grace away; threatening Darcy; throwing me out; hunting me down. I should hate him for the lifetime of hatred he has shown me, and the barbed seed he has planted in my heart: that my mammer felt the same.

I should be glad to see Dadder suffer. But I'm not. I'm too exhausted and shaken to feel anything much. I'm still reeling from the chase across the mire, and the sight of those corpses – just floating there. People, animals – suspended in the dark, stinking water . . .

I feel giddy. Mad. Aching with tiredness and wrung out like a rag.

I need to eat something.

I eat an apple and a lump of hard cheese. I collect water from the stream and make Dadder sip some of it. It runs down his unshaven chin. He slumps back into unconsciousness.

The sun rises over Gallows End – fiery orange and gold, slowly warming my shivering, sweat-drenched back. I watch the track. I am waiting for Silas to emerge from the mist, but he doesn't appear. Perhaps he has given up and turned back. Perhaps the mire took him. *Or the Marsh King.*

But then there *is* something. A shape coming towards us. I sit up. My heart gives a thud of fear – for Grace, for myself . . . The shape becomes bigger, clearer: a grey mare. A grey mare with no rider. *Silver.*

I swallow hard.

Jet lifts his tired head. Flint trots to meet her, butting his head gently against her side as if he were just a little colt. He leaps about playfully, tossing his head.

Silver joins us in the grove. She is exhausted. Her legs and chest are dark with mire water. There is no sign of Silas Kirby.

Perhaps we will never see him again, I think. It is a cruel hope and I try not to dwell on it; I know it is terrible to wish death upon anyone. But I can't help thinking that if Silas really were gone for ever, things would be a lot better for my family . . . Grace could come home with no fear of being forced to wed. Flint could stay with us for ever . . .

I lie down to rest for a moment and, when I close my eyes, I imagine Silas Kirby's face, hanging there in the foul water, all blank and withered – one of hundreds of lost souls swallowed up by Sorrow Mire.

21

I wake up stiff and achy from lying on the ground. But my mind is wide awake, ticking like a cricket: *Grace, Grace, Grace* . . . The sun is red and tired, sliding down the sky over Sorrow Mire. I have slept most of the day. Evening is gathering, and I must get myself to the fayre. Tonight will be a full moon – the fayre's last night here at Gallows End – and by morning it will have gone.

I can't wait any longer to be with Grace. That sad, ragged feeling that is always inside me is more painful, more intense, than ever, and I know that being with her will help to soothe it a little – it always does. I wish I understood it: this strangeness. What it is, and where it comes from. I feel so lost, so incomplete. Out on Sorrow Mire there were moments when the fear and despair almost swallowed me up. I see now how close I came to straying from the path. What would have become of me without the map and compass? Without Flint?

But I mustn't think about any of that now. It is over – the mire, the journey. Soon I will be with Grace again.

What to do with Dadder, though?

I will decide later. I make sure he is covered with the scratchy blanket and find more wood to build up the fire. I check the map and Mister Moss's compass: the village of Gallows End can only be a mile or so from here. I will leave the horses to rest and go to the village on foot. Old Jet is standing now, tearing and munching at the long grass – he looks better than he did at dawn, faltering through the mist like a shadow.

'Good boy, Jet,' I say, giving him a pat. 'There's life in you yet, old fella.' For a moment I think about all those glances Flint gets from passers-by . . . *Would someone be bold enough to steal him?* No. Not with Dadder there snoozing by the fire; people will think he is a pedlar resting his horses. I turn back and look at the scene, and feel a twist of sympathy for Dadder. He has spent his whole life trying to be taken seriously – to be respected as a gentleman farmer. But now here he is, sleeping in a rough camp by the roadside – the same way he began.

The walk up to the village is peaceful. Gallows End is quiet and wild. It is in the furthermost top-right corner of Mister Moss's map, and that is exactly what it feels like: a faded corner, a borderland. The map ends here, and so does the Lost Marsh. Gallows End is a sliver of earth, pincered between Sorrow Mire and the ancient forest. To the south, beyond the vastness of the mire, are tidal wetlands that stretch out to meet the sea. You can smell the waves from up here: a clean salty breeziness gusting above the quaggy hum of the mire. There are gulls too – gliding on their slim wings high above, carried inland by the weather.

To the north and east, beyond Gallows End and the last gulp of Sorrow Mire, lies the ancient forest. I wonder if there are wolves in those woods; there aren't any sheep grazing here – the narrow fields are full of peas and beans and cabbage.

There is no real heart to this village. Clusters of cottages crouch together, hidden behind thickets and spinneys. I come to a crossroads, where the track I ought to have taken around the mire meets up with this one, leading on through the village. There are gallows at the crossroads – the gallows that must have given this strange place its name. Ropes dangle like vines from the old wooden frame. I don't want to look at them. I keep walking instead, straining my ears to hear the music of the fayre.

I can feel the heat of the place as I approach, the throbbing of the music and laughter. Some folk are wearing veils to keep the bitey-flies off, but most aren't – confident that the worst of the marsh fever has now passed. I keep my veil on and pull up the hood of Mammer's cloak. There is a part of me that wants to stay anonymous here. I can't shake the feeling that Silas Kirby might still appear, half-drowned – murderous and dripping with the mire, come to sentence Grace to life as his bride. But there is something else too – an uneasy feeling in the air. A sense of danger, of being watched or followed. I am sure it is all in my head – that I am just nervous, excited to see Grace.

The first thing I do is buy myself a baked apple and scoff it down. I think of it as a sort of ritual – a little bit of magic to bring Grace back – as if repeating this thing we did together will somehow untangle the mess since she ran away, whisking us back in time to that snowy December night. I imagine my sisters here with me – Grace and Freya with their golden hair gleaming in the light of all the coloured lanterns . . .

Freya.

Rage bubbles up in me at once. *Why did she tell Dadder and Silas where to find me? What on earth was she thinking?* I shake my head, trying to get rid of the rage, and all thoughts of Freya too. Freya can wait. The important thing now is to find Grace.

The fayre looks so different, though, and it isn't just that it is pitched in a different place, with quickthorn blossom on the ground instead of snow. All the tents and stalls are the same – I think – but everything is in a different place. It is like wandering through an enchanted maze, with walls that keep shifting around. Even when I stop and look back, the tents I have just passed look unfamiliar. *You're still tired*, I say to myself. *Still recovering from the marsh fever, still haunted by Sorrow Mire* . . . I try to find that feeling I had last time – freedom, fun! The three of us running like giddy goats through the colours and the cooking smoke, on our way to the big tent.

That is where I am going now. I can see its red-and-white striped walls rising up at the heart of the fayre. I am muddling my way towards it. This is where Grace will be – dancing in the big show, just as that floppy-haired boy suggested. What was his name? *Viktor.*

All these months, I have dreamt of Grace dancing here – dressed in white feathers, as an elegant swan. Or in dark blue, with fine gauze wings, trailing silk streamers from the trapeze; flitting like a damselfly far above the audience . . . *How happy she must be!* Could I be happy here too? What job would they let me do? I could never be a performer – I'm not musical like Grace; I can't sing or dance or play an instrument. Perhaps if I bring Flint, Silver and old Jet too, they will let us join the company and I can help look after all those beautiful night-black horses . . . I try to imagine these billowing silk structures as my new home. But it all feels too odd, too other. It will be different once I find Grace, though, I'm sure.

I pass the giant, and try to ignore the cold fear that blooms in the pit of my stomach at the terrible, crushing power of him: he could snap my neck with one huge hand. He grunts and bellows as he arm-wrestles a man who wants to win the barrel of rum. I'm sure it is the same barrel of rum that I saw last time. No one can defeat him.

I pass the man with the screaming monkey on his shoulder, but . . . *Didn't I pass him a few moments ago?* The music is so loud, blaring and clashing, but it seems to be coming from everywhere around me. I should be at the heart of the fayre by now – the big tent should be right here, shouldn't it?

And then it is. All of a sudden, it is as if the stalls and sideshows just melt away like monsters in a nightmare, and the big red-and-white striped tent is standing right in front of me.

My heart gives a happy little start, and I smile – I'm so nearly there, by my sister's side once more! Viktor is standing at the entrance, taking coins from three girls. I can see someone moving about just inside the tent, behind the great swagged curtain – a long purple coat, a whip. It must be Viktor's father – the showman with the white tiger. One of the three girls going in is dressed in a long, blue cloak, a bit like mine. I have a weird sense of time sliding sideways – as if I have just seen myself going in to watch the show with Grace and Freya. Viktor smiles at the girls. He mutters something to his father, who immediately vanishes. And then he turns to look straight at me. His brown eyes smile cheerly.

'Evening, miss,' he says. 'Come to see the show?'

'I'm looking for my sister, Grace,' I say. 'She's one of the dancers.'

He looks at me and frowns. 'Grace?'

A strange, cold feeling flips my insides right over.

'No Grace here, I'm afraid,' he says, shaking his head. 'We have a Gwen. Is that who you mean?'

'Grace,' I say again, as if repeating her name will change what he just said. 'My sister is called Grace. She joined the fayre just before Yule, from a village called Hollow-in-the-Marsh. You said she could come and be a dancer – you helped my other sister Freya look for us . . .'

'Ah,' he says and grins at me. 'I remember you now. Freya was very cross you left her. And I remember your other sister. Very beautiful. Grace! Yes – my father would have loved her to join the show, I'm sure. But she never did. We still are missing one dancer . . .'

'She never joined . . . *She isn't here?*' My excited, pattering heart doesn't know what to do with itself. I feel heat rising up my neck, tears starting in my eyes.

Viktor looks at me closely. 'You have come all the way from your village to find her?'

'Yes,' I gasp. 'She – she must be here. Could she have

got a different job? Perhaps she's selling food, or looking after the animals?'

Viktor shakes his head slowly and his dark hair flops
across his eyes. 'The Full Moon Fayre is small – smaller
than you would think. Everyone here knows everyone
else. If your sister Grace had joined us all those months
ago, I would know she was here. I'm sorry.'

'Then . . . where . . .?'

'I can't help you. She did not join the fayre at
Hollow-in-the-Marsh, and she isn't here now.' He nods
to a queue of people gathering behind me. 'I can see
you are upset – and I'm sorry. But I have work to do. If
I don't sell tickets to these people, my father will be
very angry . . .'

I move aside to let the people past, my mouth still
open to speak, but with nothing left to say.

I feel faint. Numb. Viktor's words start to bleed
through me, dizzying as the marsh fever. Slowly,
slowly, they find their way to my brain: *Grace isn't here.
She isn't a dancer with the Full Moon Fayre. And she never
has been.*

22

I go back through the fayre, drifting vague as the mist over Sorrow Mire. I am jostled by people, blasted by music and shrill shrieks of laughter, but I am barely aware of anything.

Grace — isn't — here.

For all these months it has been a certainty in my mind. The same as knowing there will be water in the well when I drop my bucket down into the darkness: *Grace is dancing at the Full Moon Fayre. Grace is free. Grace is happy . . .*

But she *isn't* with the fayre, and what if she isn't free or happy either?

Dadder's words to Silas Kirby come back to me: *I'll warrant she's at the bottom of a ditch somewhere . . .*

Could she be . . . *dead*? No — I'd feel that somewhere

inside, wouldn't I? I'd *know* . . .

I think back to the horrors of my lonely journey here — the spookiness of Foulfield, the funeral at Hogback Hill, all but dying of marsh fever in Frightwood, crossing Sorrow Mire and seeing those faces in the water . . . Through all that, the thought of Grace was what kept me going, but now . . .

The noise of the fayre is behind me, fading to a distant blur of music and voices. I have wandered down the hill in a sort of trance. I am back at the camp. The horses look up, and then go back to their evening grazing. Dadder's blanket is still rising and falling, rising and falling. Fast, fevered. I build up the fire and stand there, soaking up its warmth.

There is a thought batting softly at the edge of my mind, like a moth. Each time I try to catch it, it flitters away.

I gaze out at the darkness of Sorrow Mire stretching out below us — eerie, dangerous, hungry — and the thought flitters past once more, closer this time, beating its pale, papery wings.

I am thinking of the Marsh King, and the lost souls lured into the mire by his lantern. I am thinking of Gytha Greenwood in the fairy tale, of Sarah and Amos's dadder, crossing the mire and never coming home . . .

What if Grace never ran away from home at all? Or what if she tried to run away and something awful happened to her? What if she has become one of these lost souls? One of the missing.

And as soon as I think it, I feel in my bones that it is true.

The notes of Grace's lullaby drift like a dream into my mind, her voice so real I catch my breath, gasping into the darkness, straining to see her there: *A damsel slept beside a brook, a-dreamin' and a-dreamin'*...

My heart tightens. Tears are running down my face. I have used up everything that is brave and hopeful inside me. I have eked it out this far, keeping going – *I only need to get as far as the fayre* . . . And now I have nothing left.

Grace's song is soothing me, lulling me.

The sky was black, the stars were bright, the waxen moon was gleamin'.

There is a soft pink light glowing over the mire now, warm and welcoming. I feel myself drawn towards it, as if it is home – as if Grace is there, calling to me.

The rain fell soft, the sun arose, the winter was a-creepin',
But still the damsel dreamt and dreamt, a-cursed to e'er be sleepin'...

I take a few steps towards the light, but then there is a movement behind me. I jump, jolted out of the strange spell that had taken hold of me.

'May?' a voice croaks.

It is Dadder. He is sitting up, staring at me in a feverish daze. His jaw is shuddering with the fever. His face is all damp with sweat. 'May?' he says again. And then he sobs. 'My sweetheart!'

May. May was Mammer's name.

He squints at me, blinking in the brightness of the fire. I think of Freya emerging from the springtide flames — with the light burning behind her, she was just a silhouette, a shadow. My face is veiled: he can see my long, dark hair; he can see the cloak I am wearing, and the brooch too . . .

He thinks I am Mammer.

'May?' He reaches out. His hand is trembling. Tears are streaming down his crumpled face. 'I'm sorry, May,' he sobs, collapsing forward. 'I'm so sorry.'

Sorry for what?

I am frozen to the spot. I don't know what to do. *If I speak, he will know it's me . . . Or is he too mad with the fever?* I decide to risk it.

'Why are you sorry?' I say very softly.

'I told 'em. About your mammer. About Grammy.'

'Told them what?'

'I told 'em — the whole village — I told 'em about her blastin' me across the room with her magic . . .'

No . . . Please, no . . .

'It weren't my fault, May — I had to say somethin'. After Flint disappeared, they were goin' to put me in the stocks for bein' a thief! Said I must be hidin' him somewhere. They were draggin' me off to the stocks. I couldn't face it, May — the shame of it! I had to say somethin'. So I told 'em. I told 'em about Grammy's magic — that everythin' with Flint and the girls runnin' off was all *her* fault – and folks' lambs dyin' too, and that old fella's hay barn that burnt down. I said she'd put the evil eye on us all. They're all cryin' out witchery now. It's just a matter of time until—'

'Until what?' My voice is just a whisper. My hands are trembling like Dadder's, but not because of the marsh fever. Fear has hold of me – all icy and terrible.

'Just a matter of time till they come for her.'

23

Now I understand why Freya told Dadder where to find me. She needed to get me home, and setting Dadder and Silas on my trail – like great, bullish bloodhounds – was her way of doing it.

The folk of Hollow-in-the-Marsh think Grammy is a witch.

They are coming for her.

And we have to stop them.

Dadder reaches out for me once more, still sobbing and sweating. 'May,' he mumbles. 'My May . . .'

'I'm not May,' I say, and my voice is stony cold. 'I'm Willa. And we're going home. Now.'

I could leave him behind – and it is so tempting now, more tempting than ever – to let him die here by the wayside. But I need him to tell everyone that it isn't true – that Grammy isn't really a witch, that he made the whole thing up. Perhaps then they will change their minds . . . I can't bear to think about what they will do to her. *Burning?* Surely not – it has been generations since the last witch-burning in the village . . . *Flogging, then, or trial by water?*

What if I am already too late? I have to get home as soon as I can.

As I pack up my bundle, I think about the triplets and Freya – how scared they must be. I think about Missus Cooper and those others in the village who have always hated Grammy – jealous of the sway she held over the council of elders, with her different way of seeing things, her stubbornness, and her clever, sharp tongue. And that's the answer to it all. *Hate. Jealousy.* Missus Cooper has been waiting for a chance like this for years and years. With Grammy out of the way, Missus Cooper will be queen bee . . .

I leave Dadder slumped on the grass while I saddle up the horses. Jet seems strong again, thank goodness. He even dances a bit when I say, 'Home, boys. We're going home.'

I look out over Sorrow Mire. There is no fog tonight. The full moon is deathly bright: its light makes ghosts of the reed clumps and nodding bulrushes; it shines dully in each filmy, depthless puddle, as if it is trapped beneath the slimy surface.

It will be the quickest way home to Grammy . . .

But I don't think I can do it.

What if I see those drowned faces in the water? What if I see that strange light again – that will-o'-the-wisp? What if I find Silas Kirby, dead in the mud? Or worse – still alive?

No. We will take the long way around the mire tonight. I just have to hope we can get home in time to save Grammy.

I tie Jet's reins in a knot. I put the bundles across Flint's back.

I lead Silver to a half-rotten log, then I drag Dadder to his feet. 'Climb up.'

He moans and sways and says he can't, but he manages to wobble up on to the log, and then to get a boot in the stirrup. 'Let me rest,' he groans. 'Let me die.'

'You can die when you're home, and you've taken back what you said about Grammy,' I say firmly. 'And not before.'

He pulls feebly on the saddle, and I shove him hard. Eventually he is up on Silver's back. He looks around, confused, then he spies Flint.

'Oh,' Dadder grizzles. His eyes fill with tears. 'I've missed you! How I've missed my beautiful boy.'

Something buckles in my heart. *He's never spoken to me like that. Or any of us.*

I mount Flint. He feels all jumpy beneath me. I click

to Silver to follow us, then I call Jet too: 'Come on, old fella.'

Our dear old nag nods his way over and I touch my hand to his nose. 'Silver has got Dadder, Flint has got me and the bundles, so all you've got to worry about is putting one foot in front of the other. You can make it home, old boy. I know you can.'

The ride around Sorrow Mire is long, rough and winding. I lead the way on Flint, with Silver and Jet following close behind. We pass no one on the road. It is just us, and the moonlight. I want to be going faster, and Flint is itching to move quickly too, but I have to keep him steady: nothing more than a slow trot on this bumpy road, or Dadder will topple off, and poor Jet will probably collapse at the roadside.

I curse each tedious mile.

Should I have been braver? Should I just have crossed Sorrow Mire after all?

I think about my fearless little sister, Darcy, and my fingers touch the silver omlet fastening my cloak. So much for my courageous quest . . .

At last, we meet up with the track at the western end of Sorrow Mire, and we go up through the ghostly forest towards Frightwood. I rest the horses here for an hour, then set off again at dawn. The road is better here, and we push along fast and pacey. Flint and Silver have the same brisk trot. Dadder is clinging tight to the pommel, and old Jet is managing to keep up with us. He knows we are going home. He's probably thinking about his nice cosy stable and his nosebag full of oats.

I am longing for home too. But I am dreading what we will find when we get there.

I hope to reach Hogback Hill by nightfall, but then Jet starts limping, barely touching his hind left hoof to the ground, so we stop. I prise out a stone that had wedged itself in the softer part of his foot. 'We'll rest here for a bit, shall we?' I say, taking his saddle off. Jet nuzzles my shoulder, and I see that Flint is already wandering off the path. There is a donkey grazing in a field here, and Flint is trying to start races with him, up and down the fence. The donkey does not seem keen. At last Flint tosses his head in disgust and munches on the long grass of the verge instead.

I sit down with Mister Moss's map. The journey should be quicker from here. When I was heading east, I came all higgledy-piggledy across the marsh and farmland to stay off the main track, then I took a wrong turn and ended up in Foulfield. But I'm better with the compass now. If I take the most direct way back to Hollow-in-the-Marsh – the way Dadder and Silas must have come – we could be home by tomorrow evening. And we won't have to go anywhere near Foulfield, thank goodness.

I shudder.

The weirdness of that place is all meshed up inside me with the clammy fear I felt striking out alone, desperate to find my sister. And here I am returning, a month or so later, with nothing to show for it. Grace is lost, and soon Grammy may be lost too.

24

As we come into Hollow-in-the-Marsh, the sky is darkening. It's not night-time – not yet; storm clouds are filling the sky, rolling and boiling and black as ash. The wind is gathering, roaring over my ears like rushes of thunder.

I catch the sound of voices in the gusting air. I follow them, taking the track that leads home – up to our farm.

And then I see them. Everyone. The whole damn village.

They are crowding into our farmyard, chattering with excitement. 'WITCH!' someone shouts, and then others join in too: '*Witch! Witch! Witch!*'

My whole body is shaking – terrified and furious. If only I'd got home yesterday – or even a few hours ago

– perhaps Dadder could have said his piece, and we could have stopped this in time . . .

The faces of the crowd are deadly, but there is a frenzied glee in their eyes too – they are enjoying every moment. Hatred has made them into a pack. If Grammy is wicked, then they must be righteous!

'Rats,' I spit. 'You *rats*.'

I tether the horses to the gatepost, leaving Dadder slumped across Silver's shoulders. The horses are nervy, upset by the noise and movement of the mob. My own heart is banging like a funeral drum.

Grammy is still alive, I say to myself. *If they are shouting like this – she must still be alive. It's not too late – it's not too late . . .*

I pull up the hood of my cloak and start squeezing through the crowd, hoping no one notices who I am. There is a stench in the air – the smell of sweaty, excited bodies crowded together, steeped in eagerness and grog, grinding their boots into the muck of our yard.

I can see Freya on the steps, guarding the door with the wood axe in her hands. The triplets are there with her. Darcy is gripping the fire poker as if it's a sword; there is not a flicker of fear upon her round, serious face, and suddenly I realize how much she looks like Grammy.

Grammy. She must still be inside. The mob are here to take her away . . .

I squeeze through the gaps between stinking coats, ducking beneath elbows and the blades of rusty shovels. There is a strange feeling in the air – a charged-up feeling, all buzzing and dangerous. The sky above us churns and grumbles. Rain starts to fall in big, hard drops.

'*Witch! Witch! Witch!*' the crowd cry.

But then there is another voice, crying out like a stuck pig. And someone shouts, 'It's Nate – Nate Fernsby's back!' And people turn around to see him there.

'Help me,' Dadder moans. 'I'm dyin'! Help me . . .'

'What's she DONE to him?' someone screams.

'She's struck him down, that's what.' It's Missus Cooper. She is right in front of me – yards from our door – holding a flaming torch. Her eyes burn with its light: *I'm queen bee now*.

'The evil eye!' someone shouts.

'Yes,' says Missus Cooper. 'She's put the evil eye upon him!' And the crowd start babbling excitedly.

'It's her what did for those lambs,' I hear someone hissing. 'It's her what set that hay barn alight.'

They are so desperate to make sense of these losses, so desperate for someone to blame other than themselves . . .

'Grammy didn't put the evil eye on anyone,' I say loudly. 'She didn't kill any lambs or set fire to any hay barns. And Dadder's got bitten by a bitey-fly. It's marsh fever!' No one is listening to me. 'Grammy hasn't hurt *anyone*!' And then I am standing up on the steps with my sisters beside me. 'Tell them, Dadder!' I shout. 'Tell them the *truth*.'

But Dadder is lost in the misery of his fever. 'I'm dyin',' he moans again. And hands reach up to help him from Silver's back. It is no use. He is too sick to change his story, and, looking at the sea of crazed faces in front of me, I can see it is far too late to change their minds. They have waded too deep into this madness now. They *need* it to happen. They will *make* it happen, no matter what.

'Too long she's flounced about this village like she owns the place,' Missus Cooper says quietly, nudging the woman next to her: 'Time she was brought down a peg or two.'

'Fetch a horse whip!' someone else shouts.

'There'll be no whipping.' It's Elder Warren. He is pushing his way to the front of the crowd.

'*Defend* her, would you?' People are poking at him. '*Defend* the witch?'

I can see the struggle on his face. He has to give them something, or they will turn upon him too.

'The ducking stool,' he announces. His face is grim. 'Grey Brothers' Pond. First thing in the morning.'

'NOW!' they shout. 'Or she'll escape! Fetch her *now*!' The crowd push past Elder Warren, surging all at once like a tide.

But the five of us surge back at them. 'Get away from our grammy! Get AWAY from our house!' we roar, into the wind and the flaming of the torches.

There is a blinding flash in the sky above. 'GET AWAY!' we bellow, and thunder booms across the lowering skies, echoing our anger.

The crowd hesitate. They look up at the sky. They look at us. There is a whispering. 'What if it's in *them* too?' someone mutters. 'What if there's wickedness in *all* them Fernsby girls?' They start to shuffle back. Not far – they are not giving up this easily – but far enough to give us time to think.

'Inside, quick,' I breathe.

'But Dadder . . .' Dolly says. 'We can't leave him . . .'

'Get the door,' comes a voice from the yard. It's Mister and Missus Moss, and Fergus too – they are carrying Dadder by the arms and legs.

I hold the door open, watching the crowd like a sheepdog watching a wolf pack. Mister and Missus Moss and Fergus carry Dadder across the kitchen and put him on his box bed by the fire. We all move into the house and bolt the door behind us. Fergus helps Freya to wedge a heavy chair against it, then he and his dadder go through the house, barricading the other doors and windows.

We all stand still for a second. Breathing hard and looking at each other.

Then there is a voice from the chair beside the fire: 'Willa!'

'Grammy!' I rush to her, fall to my knees, and bury my face in her soft shoulder. I sob and sob and sob, and she rubs my back. 'Ah, Willa,' she says gently. 'You're home now.'

I want to be a little girl again, giving myself up to the safety of Grammy's arms, but the horror of the mob is shuddering through me: 'We won't let them take you, Grammy – we won't let them!'

She holds me away a little. 'What did Elder Warren say? The stocks? The gaol?'

We shake our heads. 'The ducking stool,' Freya says quietly.

We are all silent, all thinking the same thing. *Splosh, GASP, splosh, GASP* . . .

'Well, that's that, then.' Grammy smiles. 'And I had a feeling it would be. My chest won't stand it. In and out o' that cold water fifty times or more. It'll be the death of me.'

'Grammy—'

'It's all right, my chickens. This day's bin comin' for years – I've bin waitin' for it.' She puts one hand over her heart. 'I'm failin' now. Can't get my breath like I used to. Pains in here. Terrible pains. An old lady's got to go sometime.'

'No, Grammy – not like this . . .'

'And why not, I ask you? What a way to go! People

will talk about it for generations – The Witch of Hollow-in-the-Marsh! I'll be a legend to your grand-children and to their grandchildren too – just like one of the stories in your mammer's book – like the Greenwood sisters! How about that, eh? I'm not afraid. And if I'm not afraid, you mustn't be either. Any of you.'

There is a drumming from outside. Rain batters the roof. Boots and shovels pound upon the ground in time with their whooping and chanting. But Grammy isn't paying the slightest bit of attention.

'Now,' she says, mopping a tear from my cheek with her hanky, and cupping my chin in her hand. 'Did you find Grace?'

I tell her everything, as quickly as I can. Grammy's fire-bright eyes are fixed on me, and so are the eyes of my sisters.

'She wasn't at the fayre,' Grammy breathes. 'But . . . You think you know where she is?'

'Not exactly,' I say, lowering my voice. 'But do you remember that story about the Marsh King in Mammer's book? You said his spirit still haunted the mire, gathering lost souls . . .'

'Aye. But that's a fairy tale, my chicken. A way of thinking about things.'

'I know, but what if . . .?'

'What if . . .?' Dolly echoes, watching me with enormous eyes. Deedee's stubby fingers touch my arm. She nods and whispers, 'What if . . .?'

Freya is waiting too, and the Mosses.

Grammy finishes my sentence for me: 'What if Grace is a lost soul?'

I nod.

No one knows what to say.

Grammy thinks about it for a moment. 'Well. All stories have to start somewhere, don't they? Maybe once there really was a tyrant king who ruled the Lost Marsh – who ruled with fear, and druv the people like cattle. Fear like that has a power all of its own, you know. It haunts a place. Seeps into the earth and into people's hearts, like the chill of the mire.'

She looks towards the box bed where Dadder is shuddering with fever. Missus Moss is holding a cup of water to his lips.

'But the Marsh King hisself?' I whisper. 'And the souls he has taken?'

The voices outside are getting louder, louder, closing in. *WITCH, WITCH, WITCH!*

Grammy turns to the door, then turns back to me and smiles. 'You've bin lookin' for trouble all your life, Willa Fernsby, and perhaps now we know why. You'll find Grace. I know you will. Perhaps she *is* lost somewhere out there. And if she is, you'll find her. Just remember – even when you feel small and helpless and you think you're all by yourself – you aren't. Not a bit of it. You're stronger than you think.

And you are never truly alone.'

I sniff and nod.

Grammy wipes my cheek with her pinny. 'I wish we had more time, Willa. There are things I should have told you long ago, but . . .' She trails off and shakes her head. Then she kisses my forehead. 'I don't think that rabble will wait any longer. And I don't want 'em kickin' the door down or settin' fire to the place.' She sighs. 'Pass me that stick.' She nods to the long pole that lies along the wall by the door. It's the one I used to clear the snow off the roof. She grips it and gets to her feet. She must be more frail than I thought. She hobbles across the kitchen, suddenly ancient and wizened. The tallness of the stick makes her look even smaller.

'Grammy, you can't let them take you.'

'Don't be ridiculous,' she snaps. 'I'm not lettin' anyone take me anywhere. I'm goin' of my own free will.' She spins around to face us all. 'That's what it's about, girls – that's what it is *all* about. Folks here are afraid of free will. Afraid of someone who asks questions, who wants to rewrite the way things are. Goodness knows, it's bin a battle between me and your dadder. But promise me something. Every one of you. You won't be druv by other folks, with their superstitions an' their curses. The Fernsby girls will stand together and they won't be druv – not by fear, not by nobody. Promise?'

'We promise,' we say, and Darcy salutes.

'We – won't – be – druv,' Dolly and Deedee chant together, marching on the spot. I don't think they have the slightest clue what Grammy is talking about.

Grammy smiles. 'It's there in every one of you. That *fire*. People won't like it when they see it in you. But never let them put it out. Not ever.'

We nod.

Thunder crashes right overhead, and my heart crashes against my ribs.

'Couldn't be better!' Grammy smiles, raising her eyes towards the storming heavens. 'Couldn't be better . . . I'm ready.'

Freya and I look at each other. *We should try to stop her.*

But there is no stopping Grammy. She yanks the chair away from the door and flings it open. She stands there, framed in the black doorway, tinier than ever, wrapped up in her bright-coloured shawls, clutching the snow-pole as if it's a wizard's staff.

The crowd fall silent.

'There'll be no shovin' and no nonsense, and you won't be carryin' me on your shoulders like a scare-crow to a bonfire, so don't even think about it,' she says firmly. 'If anyone so much as lays a finger on me, I shall strike him down with magic and turn him into a toad.'

They are all watching her. Nobody moves.

'Well, come on, then,' Grammy says cheerfully. 'Why are you all just standing there? Let's get on with it.'

25

The procession moves through the village like a twisting, flaming serpent. Missus Cooper leads the way with her torch. Elder Warren is scuttling along at her side. Others have torches too. They spit and sizzle in the rain.

The sky above is a cauldron – churning, crackling with darkness.

We walk alongside Grammy – we will not let anyone else near her. I don't know what she is doing, playing along with this horror show. All I know is I am not leaving her side. *Stand together*, Grammy said. And we are. Freya and I flank Grammy on one side, Dolly and Deedee on the other. Darcy is in front, still wielding the fire poker, stretching out her skinny little legs to keep pace with the rushing crowd.

The rabble are bubbling, babbling. A boy behind us whispers to his brother: 'I heard she has books in her house! *Books*!'

'Aye, *books*!' Grammy says over her shoulder, and they jump nearly out of their skins. 'Well, p'raps there *are* books in my house, lads. P'raps there're books in quite a few houses hereabouts, only folks are too scared to let on.'

She stops. Everyone behind her stops too. 'Because you do have brains in those heads of yours, lads, and you do have good hearts too – I know you do. It's the easiest thing in the world to lose your way, to get swept along with something cruel—'

'Enough of that,' Missus Cooper interrupts loudly. 'It's that sort of high-horse nonsense that's got you in this pickle!'

Grammy smiles. 'Ah. So I need humblifyin', do I? That's what it's all about. You want to shame me. Well, shame on *you*, Missus Cooper. Shame on *you*.'

We are at the foot of Glorious Hill now, at Grey Brothers' Pond. The water is deep and cold and black. The old ducking stool that hides here amongst the willow trees has always reminded me of a giant see-saw. But now it looks like something else entirely. It looks like gallows.

Rain is splattering down on to the wet turf, coursing into the swollen pond.

Missus Cooper draws herself up like a proud old

pigeon. 'Is the duckin' stool ready?' she demands.

It is.

The crowd are all jostling to find their places on the bank of the pond. No one wants to miss this.

The sky above rumbles dangerously. The rain falls harder, dripping down on us through the drooping canopy of the willow trees.

Missus Cooper and two of her gramsons come for Grammy. Joss is one of them – Grace's Green Man. His head is down. He won't look any of us in the eye.

But Grammy pushes past them. 'No need to herd me,' she says. 'I'm not a sheep.' She starts hobbling up the hill, away from the ducking stool.

'Where's she goin'?'

She spins around. 'I am goin' to pay my respects to my ancestors.' She gestures to the trees on the far slope of Glorious Hill. 'Goin' to say farewell.'

'Farewell?' Missus Cooper mocks. 'This is a ducking, Grammy Whittle – it isn't an execution.'

Grammy raises her eyebrows at her old enemy. *Isn't it?*

'Of course it's not . . .' But Missus Cooper's voice is drowned out by the baying of the crowd.

'Throw her in the water! Burn her! *Witch! Witch! Witch!*'

Missus Cooper looks around at her friends, her neighbours, and the expression on her face changes.

Grammy hobbles up the hill – she is climbing the steeper, treeless slope, the side the triplets like to roll down on sunny days.

The crowd are going after her now – fanning out through the tall, wet grass, but not daring to get too close – watchful and wary as wolves. Their torches flicker and sizzle in the rain.

Grammy hobbles on, using the stick and gaining ground like a little low creature – using up every bit of life and strength left in her old bones.

Is she really going to pay her respects to her ancestors? Or is she up to something? I can't help hoping she will find a way to turn the tables on them yet . . .

The sky overhead crackles strangely. There is an extraordinary feeling in the air – a fizzing and tingling. My skin is prickling all over, every hair standing on end. Grammy is scrambling up the slope. So many of her family are buried up there – her husband, her own parents, her daughter . . . She stops short of the trees though, and stands stock-still on the bare mound at the top of Glorious Hill. It is the highest point for miles around.

She is such a small figure up there – round as a ball and all swaddled up, holding tight to her tall wizard's staff . . .

What on earth is she doing?

She is just standing there, looking up into the black, crackling sky.

The air buzzes. There is an immense flash of light – a bright, jagged bolt connecting Grammy to the boiling clouds.

It blinds us all for a moment, and then it is gone. Thunder crashes above our heads again. Rain pours down – everything blurs.

'What happened? *What happened?* Where is she?'

'She's gone! She's disappeared! Black magic! *Witchery!*'

But she hasn't disappeared, and it wasn't witchery.

It was lightning.

A vein of smoke hangs in the air above the mound. I blink and blink in the rain. I can't see Grammy or her stick. I can't see anything but a violent shape of light, burnt into my eyes by the lightning. I am running up the meadow towards the mound, my four sisters pant-ing behind me. '*Grammy!*'

And there she is. Just a tiny shape, collapsed upon the ground. A pile of bright rags.

The long stick is smouldering in the grass – flung from her hand by the force of the lightning.

I kneel down, cradling her head in my hands. Her long silver plait lies across my lap.

Tears are pouring down my face. 'Grammy?'

Her eyes are closed.

Darcy is here, gently holding the hand that held the pole. The palm is blackened.

Freya is beside me. 'Grammy? Grammy!'

But her limbs are limp. Her chest is not rising and

falling. Her face and neck are blazoned with a deep, flaming scar, jagged as the lightning that struck her . . .

She is dead.

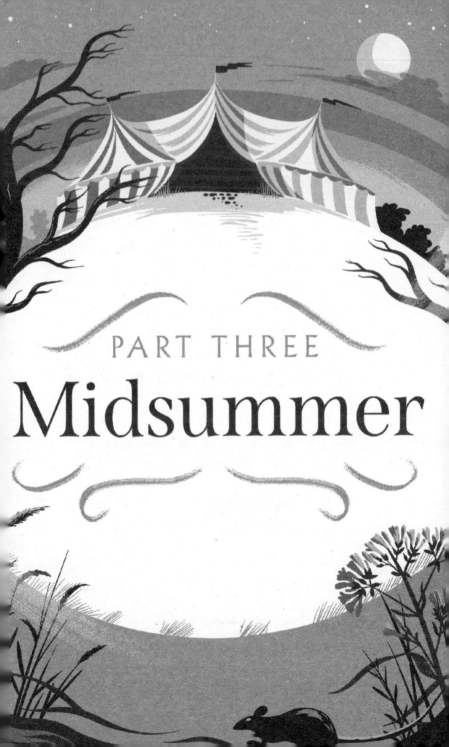

PART THREE

Midsummer

May blossomed and the corn grew tall. Hay swayed in the meadows, ripe for scything. The days lengthened towards midsummer like a dog stretching in the afternoon sun, and the marshes shone like gold.

May Fernsby, 'The Marsh King', *Tales of the Marshes*

26

We buried Grammy on the very spot where the lightning struck her down.

Mammer's grave is marked with a sweet-chestnut tree, and we planted an elder for Grammy. No one else came to the funeral except the Mosses, though some of the villagers were there, standing a little way down the hill. Their hands were folded in respect, their heads were bowed. Elder Warren had come to the farmhouse the very next day, and Missus Cooper was there behind him: 'We never meant to . . . It was just meant to be . . .'

It was meant to be *humblifyin'* – just as Grammy had said. But she wasn't one to be humblified, our grammy. Proud and practical to the end, she refused to give herself up to the rabble. She refused to lose her last breaths in Grey Brothers' Pond.

Did she know the lightning would strike the mound at the top of the hill? Did she choose for that to happen? I don't know. But one way or another, Grammy wrote her own ending. And what an ending. As she said, people will talk about it for years.

The sun shone down on Glorious Hill, and we sang for Grammy: 'To the earth, to the earth, to the earth that fed you; to the arms of the earth that gave you life . . .' We placed flowers in her grave – marsh marigolds, forget-me-nots, ragged robin. And we planted seeds too, around the elder sapling. When we patted down the crumbs of soil into a smooth mound, Darcy said, 'A flower bed.'

Yes. A flower *bed*.

'Sleep tight, Grammy.'

'Don't let the marsh bugs bite.'

'Dream of nice things now.'

We held hands. Five sisters about Grammy's grave, and I have never missed Grace as much as I missed her then. Darcy was holding my hand, and her little grave-muddy fingers squeezed mine tightly. *How is it possible to bear such a loss? How can we go on with this hole torn through the middle of our world? Surely everything will ebb away now, swirling and disappearing, sucked down into the black mud of the mire. It will be the end of us. The end of everything . . .*

*

Over the weeks that followed, the village watched us from afar. Some were ashamed, like Elder Warren and Missus Cooper, and those who had come to Glorious Hill to pay their respects and join in the singing. They felt the weight of that terrible night upon their shoulders. They had dismissed Dadder's accusations of witchery: *Why would they take the word of a drunkard over the word of a respected elder like Grammy?* But there were still some who clung to their dark superstitions, who believed Grammy had used magic to escape her punishment. And we felt their eyes upon us . . .

Even now, we feel watched when we go down to the village to collect water from the well. Children hide and giggle behind the quickthorn hedges, then run away, screaming. Folk stop talking when we come by; then they lean their heads close: *What happened to Silas Kirby?* they whisper. *Set off with Nate Fernsby and never come back. They've got his horses now, though — both of 'em! Flint* and *Silver. Must've done him in . . .* In some of the whispers, Dadder is the villain — a debtor who killed Silas and left his body to rot by the roadside. In other whispers, *I* am the one who murdered Silas, and Dadder is just another one of the witch's victims — one of *our* victims . . .

Dadder is not dead. Not yet. We can all see it won't be long, though. He lies in his box bed, facing the wall. He whimpers in his sleep. The marsh fever has passed at last, but it has riddled him right through, like woodworm. What's left of him is crumbling away before our eyes. He doesn't eat. His face is all sunken and grey. You can see the bones and the veins twist around each other when he moves his wrists.

It is like having a ghost here in the corner of the kitchen. We are all horribly aware of him while we cook and clean and scrub the table and eat our supper. We are silent much of the time when we are downstairs. We don't want him to hear the things we need to say, so we don't say anything at all. It is not a good silence. It is too full of grief and anger and the wishing of our broken hearts . . .

I think about Grammy all the time. I think about what she said – that she was sure I would find Grace.

Late one night I whisper to Freya from my bed. 'Do you believe in the Marsh King, Freya?'

'Nope. Go to sleep.'

'Do you remember . . . Do you remember that mark on Grammy – the way the lightning burnt her – right down the middle of her?'

Freya sighs. 'Well?'

'I've bin thinking about it. What if it means something? Grammy said it might be another sundered soul that defeats the Marsh King and saves all the lost souls he has taken. And the lightning *sundered* Grammy didn't it?'

There is a silence.

'Grammy is dead, Willa.'

'I know that . . .'

'She's not coming back, and she's not going to be fightin' any evil marsh sprites.' Freya's voice is kinder than usual.

We are both quiet. I think perhaps Freya has gone to sleep when suddenly she says, 'And, if you think about it, we're all sundered, aren't we? Every one of us. We're sundered at birth from our mothers, and sundered from those we love by distance and by death. All of us're sundered somehow. It doesn't mean we're broken, and it doesn't mean we're alone.'

'Blimey, Freya. That's awful wise.'

'I have my moments.'

I smile in the darkness.

'Actually, it was somethin' Grammy said,' she confesses.

I smile again.

'Darcy was asking about the Marsh King story one night. While you were away.'

So the Marsh King story has crept into Darcy's head too.

I can't stop thinking about it. The story is more real to me now than anything that has happened since I returned to the village. More real than Grammy's death. I know the Marsh King's spirit is out there in the mire somewhere, luring folk with his false flame, gathering lost souls . . . Grammy was so sure I could find Grace and bring her home. But how can you find someone when you don't know where to start looking?

I can't sleep. The sun has still not set – the days are warming, lengthening. Soon it will be the longest day. Midsummer. They are already building up the Midsummer Fires on the green.

I lie awake for hours as the sky fades from gold to black. I am thinking about it all, going around and around in my head, lost in the fog of my own thoughts. I think about what Freya said about sundered souls. Does that mean everyone feels like I do? That everyone feels like a part of them is missing? That they are ripped apart inside, raw with loneliness?

Dadder is groaning in his sleep. Every time he makes noises like that, I think it is the end at last. I go downstairs with my candle.

He is barely conscious. He is muttering to himself, counting on his skeleton fingers: 'Be sure the first girl marries well, the second in the home to dwell. A third maid can do little harm if set to work upon the farm . . .' And he laughs sourly. 'Hah. Little harm . . . *Little harm.*'

He turns his head suddenly, to look me in the eye. His face is foul with hatred. His breath stinks of death: 'You *cuckoo*, Willa Fernsby,' he croaks. '*You* did this to me.'

27

Dadder's words poison my dreams. *You cuckoo. You cuckoo daughter.*

I lie there, wide awake.

And then I can't stop that cruel thought creeping back; that fear that has slipped into my soul, sly as a knife . . . The words Dadder hurled at me the night I ran away: that Mammer hated me just like he did.

I want to ask Grammy. I want to ask why I am a cuckoo, and if Mammer thought it too. I've wanted to ask Grammy a hundred different things every day since the night she died. *How much honey do you put in the honey cake? Where do you keep the big darning needle? . . . Why did you leave us?*

The next morning, as soon as I have cleared the breakfast things, I go up the stairs, into Grammy's room and close the door. I breathe deeply – the comforting smell of Grammy: water-mint and soap-wort. I wonder how long the smell will last. We must keep the door closed. Keep that sweet, soft smell in here for as long as we can.

We have not touched anything in Grammy's room. Her new-washed skirts are still hanging on a line strung up across the eaves, though they dried long ago.

I go to the window. The triplets are splashing and shouting in the farmyard. I am glad. They need moments like this – away from the haunted silence of the kitchen. Sent outside to gather eggs, they are wearing the baskets as helmets and playing knights, jousting with broom handles. It isn't that they don't miss Grammy, that they aren't affected by Dadder rotting away in his box bed like a foul old turnip; it is just that they are children. They are sad one moment – they cry and cling to you – and the next moment they are silly as kittens again.

I watch Darcy, lying flat on her back in the mud, laughing so hard she can't get up. Extraordinary little person. She has taken to wearing her hair in a long plait, and it is hard not to see her as a miniature version of Grammy. The same dark sparkle in her eyes. The same uncanny, unpredictable mixture of playfulness and wisdom.

I ache for Grammy. And Grace. And Mammer.

You will never be alone, Grammy said to me the

night she died.

But I *feel* alone. Even with the noise of the triplets now, or with Freya asleep in the bed next to mine, I feel so utterly and completely alone – more now than ever before.

'What does he mean, Grammy?' I whisper. 'What does Dadder mean – that I'm a cuckoo, that's it's all my fault?'

I wait. Half-expecting a voice to come from behind me, as it so often did – when you didn't know Grammy was there. But there is no voice. Nothing at all. I open the window to let a breath of air in, and her skirts move gently in the warm breeze, swinging on the line: dancing slowly, back and forth.

I go to the secret book cupboard. None of us has been in here since Grammy died. None of us has read a word. I think we feel that reading is somehow to blame for Grammy's death. If she hadn't known how to read and write, if she hadn't taught us how to do it, perhaps she would still be alive. And there's something else too: the secret library is *hers*; it feels wrong to touch the books without her permission.

But if Grammy's soul is to be found anywhere in this house, it will be in here, with her precious books. And I need to feel close to her.

I open the cupboard. And I draw my breath in sharply.

Everything has been rearranged. All the clothes are

folded up at the very back of the cupboard, and the books have been moved to the front – just *there* – all brazen, for anyone to see – not hidden away at all. I think about what Grammy said to those young lads on the way to the ducking stool. She had already decided. It was time to stop hiding these things away. Time to stop being afraid.

The books have been arranged into piles – six piles of books. Labelled with our six names. On top of each pile is a small cloth bag. I pick up the card that says WILLA, and trace the shape of the blue-ink letters with my finger. I have so rarely seen my name written down: it makes me feel more real. I pick up my pile of books and the little cloth bag and sit down on the bed. The bag clinks softly. Money. I tug the string open and peer inside. Not just money . . .

Gold.

My heart stutters.

Grammy has divided up her books between us, and she has given each of us a little bag of gold.

Where on earth the money came from, I don't know. Grammy always had plenty of coins in her scraps bag, and she always did the totting up after market days, when we sold wool and lambs and hay . . . She must have been squirrelling her gold away all these years, so we would have something when she'd gone. Enough to stand on our own twelve feet.

And there is something else too. A thought that is

prickling the back of my mind. She *knew* she was going to die. She had prepared everything.

I look through the books in my pile – all my favourites. The one at the top is the one I was reading just before Grace disappeared. The one about the dancing princess . . . It falls open at the page I was reading last, and there, pressed between the printed pages, is a letter – all folded up and written in sky-blue ink. A letter to me.

From Grammy.

Dearest Willa,
There is something you should have been told many years ago . . .

28

His name was Colt. Colt Fernsby. He was born a few minutes after you. Your brother. Your twin.

'A boy?' your mammer cried. 'Nate will be so glad.'

And he heard – your dadder – through the tight-closed bedroom door.

'A boy!' You could hear his whoops of joy all the way down the lane to the alehouse.

But Colt was a thin little scrappit of a babby. Somehow you got all the nourishing in your mammer's tum, and he didn't get enough. No one's fault. That's just nature's way sometimes, with twins. When he saw the two of you side by side in the cradle, tangled up like pink grubs, your dadder said, 'She's a cuckoo, that one. A cuckoo chick. Look – she's fat as a squab, and my boy's all but wasted away. She'll turf him out of the nest and guzzle all the food herself.'

'Don't be silly, Nate,' I chided him. 'A lovely, healthy girl! Dark like May, and strong too. See how tight she's gripping my thumb.'

But he didn't see. He didn't want to see. Fool that he was. Nate had always wanted a lad. A lad who would inherit the farm and prosper, bringing greatness to the Fernsby name at last. Nate wanted his name to live on so that _he_ might live on. He was blind to the blessings he had been given.

Little Colt opened his eyes just once, and I'll never forget – deep, deep brown they were, dark and shining. He perished, just a few days after he'd been born – as we could all see he would. His little heart, I think. Some lambs just aren't strong enough. It's terrible sad, but there's nothing that can be done.

Your dadder drowned his grief with grog that night, and that's when it all started. Five years later, the triplets came along, and your mammer died. And that's when he decided the world was against him. That's when the superstitions took hold and he started to become a shadow of himself.

He was a jolly lad once, your dadder. Not kind – he never was kind – but he was jolly, and that's what your mammer fell for – the life in him. When he played the fiddle, you couldn't help but jig and sing. I wish you'd heard him play the fiddle, Willa. Grace might remember – it must be where the music in her comes from, after all. Be sure to ask her, when you find her. And you will find her, Willa – our warrior. I know you will.

You've been gone just over a month now. You're out there somewhere in the Lost Marsh, looking for Grace, and how I hope you've found each other!

All manner of trouble is brewing here in the village now, and I can see it won't end well.

I'll be going soon, one way or another. My chest is bad, Willa. I've known for some time. I can't catch my breath. I can't so much as feed the chickens without stopping for a rest. When your time is up, it's up. When I go, it shall be the passing of a happy old woman who has been blessed many times over. I just hope I can hold out long enough to see you safely home.

No one is ever truly gone, Willa. Your mammer – my May – she's in the bones of you. And I am too. And all the mothers who have come before us. We will never be far away. I promise. We'll be in the earth beneath your feet. In the rain that falls.

Love always,
Your Grammy

The skirts sway gently above my head. Shrieks of laughter drift in through the open window as the triplets continue their jousting. I can hear Freya too, trying to scold them into doing something useful. Flint whinnies and stamps in his stable, waiting for me to brush him, or for the triplets to plait his white tail and tell him how handsome he is. Morning light fills the room, summer-gold and dusty with pollen. But it is all quite separate from me. Quite distant.

I am still sitting on Grammy's bed, holding her letter tightly. And sitting here beside me is the ghost of my brother, Colt Fernsby.

Or not the ghost of him, but the empty space where he ought to have been. My twin. My other half. I have always been aware of this emptiness in me, this raw loneliness, but I have never understood it until now.

And this is why Dadder hates me, why I am his cuckoo daughter: he thinks it is my fault that he never had a son. No, it's worse than that — he thinks I *killed* his son.

I place Grammy's letter back between the pages. I put my books and bag of gold in the cupboard along with all the others. I leave the room, closing the door softly behind me. I go down the stairs, and sit on the edge of Dadder's box bed. He is sleeping, I think. Or, at least, he is not awake: drifting just beneath the surface of consciousness, like those faces floating in Sorrow Mire. His breathing is shallow, noisy. He does not have long now.

'I know,' I say quietly, 'about Colt. Grammy left me a letter. You should have told me years ago.'

He opens his eyes – just a crack – and peers out at me.

'It wasn't my fault that he died,' I say. I am not expecting him to agree with me, but I need to say it out loud. It is too late to argue about it, too late for apologies or forgiveness. But I am going to say what needs to be said.

'I'm sorry he died. I'm sorry I never had a brother. But it wasn't my fault. It wasn't anyone's fault. It's just a very sad thing that happened.'

He doesn't say anything at all.

'A daughter is not worth less than a son,' I say.

He blinks.

And I say it again, harder this time, tears burning my eyes, the words aching like grief in my throat: 'A daughter is not worth less than a son!'

He moves his head very slightly. Blinks again. The whites of his eyes are yellowing, shot through with tiny red lines, all jagged like the lightning that sundered Grammy.

His bony hand moves across the blanket and covers mine. I can't help but flinch at his touch. His eyes are looking past me now, up to the shelf above the fireplace – a row of old pots and tankards and dust-covered things.

'You want me to get something for you?'

His head moves again and he makes a noise in his throat. *Ar. Up there.*

I stand on a chair to reach the shelf. Here, at the very back, hidden behind Grammy's pots and jars, is an old fiddle.

'This?'

Yes, his eyes say. *Yes!*

I take it down carefully, wipe off the thick dust with a cloth.

His bony hands are stretching out, trembling. I place the fiddle on his chest and he holds it. Tears are running down his face.

'Do you want to play it?' I ask. 'Where is the bow?'

He shakes his head. He swallows. 'Gone,' he manages to say. 'To the earth. With Colt.'

He buried the bow with my brother.

I think about the graves on Glorious Hill. The taller trees have been there for fifty years and more. Then there is Grammy's elder sapling, Mammer's sweet chestnut . . . Oh! My special place there on the mound – where I feel peaceful, whole.

'The horse chestnut?' I say. 'That's where Colt is buried?'

'Ar.' More tears are squeezing from Dadder's tight-shut eyes. His fingers are moving on the broken strings of the fiddle. He can hear the old music in his head.

I want to leave him alone with his music and his

grief, but I know this may be my last chance.

'Dadder,' I say. 'I know you can hear me. There's one more thing I need to say to you. It's important.'

He opens his eyes again.

'Darcy didn't kill Mammer,' I say. 'She was a baby, not a demon. She didn't curse our family.'

'Darcy . . .' he whispers hoarsely. There is no sound to his voice. There is no breath behind it. 'Get – Darcy.'

So I do.

'Dadder wants to see you, Darcy,' I call, standing in the open doorway. The triplets stop still like statues. They look at me with open mouths. Freya pokes her head out of the chicken house. 'Dadder wants to see *Darcy?*'

My littlest sister walks solemnly to the house, takes the egg basket off her head, and drops her jousting broom by the step. She dusts off her pinny, wipes her boots on the mat, and walks to Dadder's bed. I know he is too weak to harm her now, but I still follow her, close as a shadow. I won't let his last act be a cruel one. I won't let it happen.

'Here,' he growls, beckoning her with his bony fingers.

She does not hesitate. She goes straight to his bedside and looks him right in his yellowing eyes. 'Yes?'

'Closer . . .'

My stomach tightens.

Darcy leans down towards him.

He strains up to her. He whispers something in her ear.

She steps back from the bed and looks at him for a moment. Then she says, quite simply, 'Yes, Dadder. I will bury you. Just as the curse says.'

29

Dadder's final hours were peaceful, content. Darcy was the only one he wanted near him. He would only sip water when she held the cup to his lips. After years of despising her – *fearing* her – she became the only one he trusted. He befriended her, in the way that the dying sometimes do befriend the Reaper. She was his ferryman: the one to deliver him into the next world.

We bury him on Glorious Hill. I choose a spot looking out over Hollow Mire, not too far from the young horse-chestnut tree. My twin's grave. I touch the slender trunk of his tree with my fingertips. *Hello, Colt.*

'Just here,' I say to the others, knowing Dadder would have wanted to be close to his son.

Two funerals in as many months, but this one is so

different from Grammy's. Darcy digs the hole alone. There is only one shovel, and she will not let us touch it. It takes all day. A wren sings in a hawthorn nearby – its notes pure and insistent: strong as a vow; bright as sunshine on wind-riffled water.

'So it come true,' Deedee mutters to Dolly. 'The curse. I told you it would, Dolly. Grace didn't marry Mister Kirby, an' Willa left the farm, so the curse come true – the sixth daughter is burying Dadder stone dead.'

'Don't be a ninny, Dee. The curse is just supersti-tion.' Darcy's voice comes from deep within the pit she is digging, sharp as the blade of her shovel. 'It's only come true 'cause Dadder asked me to bury him, and I said yes. I *chose* to make it come true. It's nothing to do with a silly old curse: it's me. My choice.'

'I think he wanted to be *right* about something,' I say quietly. 'All those years of Grammy telling him he was a fool. Now he'll be saying, *I told you! I told you I were right about that curse!* And he'll be happy at last.'

Freya nods. 'He was peaceful at the end.'

'He was. And that's all down to Darcy.'

We place the fiddle on his chest. We fill the grave with earth. We plant a blackthorn to mark his resting place. We sing the words we are supposed to sing. I am not singing them for the man who hated me – the man who sold my sister and threw me out of my home. I am singing them for the man who once played his fiddle and made my mammer happy.

After it is finished, we all turn towards each other. No – that's not quite right – they all turn towards me . . . The early evening sun is gold and low, shining on the faces of my sisters. Dolly and Deedee, bright-eyed as rabbits; fierce little Darcy, clutching her shovel and smirched with earth from head to foot; Freya, like a warrior queen defeated in battle, crushed beneath the weight of everything that has been on her shoulders. They turn to me because I am the one who has ventured out into the world alone. I am the one who survived and returned – scarred and broken and stronger than before. *What now?* their faces say. *What happens now?*

But, for once, I have nothing to say. I feel hollow as a scarecrow. I don't know what has happened to all that strength and stubbornness, all that fight in me. It is as if it has been buried along with Dadder's corpse. For so long now, I have been shaped by his hatred of me, spurred along by anger and confusion and bitterness. *Who am I now he has gone? Am I still a cuckoo child? The odd one out? The only one of us who is responsible for the death of another?*

I turn away to hide my tears from the others.

I sit down, grip handfuls of grass in my fists. I blink back the tears, looking up into the leaves of Mammer's sweet-chestnut tree. They are bright green, like fingers reaching out to touch the leaves of the horse chestnut growing close by, where my brother is buried. *What if Dadder was right? What if Mammer thought I was a cuckoo daughter? What if she blamed me for Colt's death too?*

I feel Freya's touch on my shoulder. 'We'll leave you here for a bit, shall we?' she says.

'Aye,' I manage to say.

'You'll bring Flint back?'

'Aye.'

Flint helped us carry Dadder here from the farmhouse, and now he is grazing at the bottom of the hill by Grey Brothers' Pond.

Darcy kisses my cheek. She smells of leaves and rain and summer earth. 'Are you all right, Willa?'

I nod, wiping my cheek on my sleeve. 'I'll be all right. We all will. I promise.' But I can't look at her.

I hear them troop off down the hill. They are talking about the farm. All the jobs that need doing. The hay is high and ready for a first mowing. It has that ripple on it when the breeze moves like fingers across the field.

'I'll ask Fergus and Mister Moss to bring their scythes and help,' Freya is saying. 'We won't get much help from the village this year. We'll just have to manage . . .'

Darcy says something about sheep shearing. Dolly and Deedee are excited about going to market. They are playing at farms like we did as babbies. But it isn't a game, and it won't be easy. Most folk in Hollow-in-the-Marsh don't trust us now – we are the gramdaughters of a witch, after all.

Their voices fade as they wander down the hill, Darcy dragging the shovel behind her. They are moving on from this moment already, thinking about the days to come – the Midsummer dancing, the harvest . . . But I am stuck. And I know I will be stuck until I find Grace.

I don't just miss her; I *need* her.

We all need her – her warmth, her good sense, her motherly ways that held us gently in our best selves. And she isn't the least bit witchy. People listen to Grace because they want to, not because she makes them.

Freya rubs folk up the wrong way and she knows it. And I go about everything like a fox in a henhouse. We need Grace to save us. But before she can do that, we need to save *her*.

I thought I knew her so well. I thought I could read her. I know she was frightened that night – terrified – of the life that lay before her. But that moment when Viktor said they needed a dancer at the fayre, I could have sworn she was thinking, *Yes. This is how I escape!*

When we woke up the next morning and found she had run away, I was *sure* she had gone with the fayre.

But she wasn't there.

She is lost now. Lost or *taken*.

The Marsh King has her soul.

I know no one else believes that apart from me. *It's just a story*, they say. But what if it isn't just a story?

I tell myself the whole tale in my head. I know it off

by heart. Mammer's words have seeped into my brain, my blood. I think about the sisters who dared to stand up to the Marsh King, Gloria and Gytha Greenwood . . . My fingers rake the cool grass. They spread out and press their tips into the ground, searching for something – digging like roots into the soft earth of Glorious Hill. *Glorious Hill.* Something jolts in my head. My fingers freeze. My eyes open wide. *Oh!*

What if it isn't Glorious Hill at all?

What if it is Gloria's *Hill?*

It is an understanding so huge that the whole world shifts around me, and I know it will never be the same as it was before.

Gloria's Hill.

The truth shivers from my fingertips all the way through me, and I believe it – I believe it with all my heart. The body of Gloria Greenwood lies somewhere beneath me. This is where Gytha buried the sister she loved. The Greenwood sisters were real, and they lived here in Hollow-in-the-Marsh.

And if they are real, then that means the Marsh King is real too.

My heart is beating like butterfly wings. The Marsh King has Grace. *How do I find him?* He could be anywhere in the whole of the Lost Marsh, haunting any of the seven mires – wandering, hiding, playing his tricks; using dark magic to lure the lost and the frightened.

The sun is setting over Hollow Mire. Golden-pink on the horizon, fading up into an eerie, poisoned grey. There is something moving on the track across the distant marsh – a shadow. A shape. A horse? Yes. Several horses. Black horses, and carts, and caravans . . .

The Full Moon Fayre has returned.

There is a juddering deep in my chest. Like fear. Like fate.

What if Viktor was wrong? my mind whispers. *What if Grace is there after all?* I watch the fayre approaching – quiet and shimmering as a nightmare.

Where better for the Marsh King to hide his magic, I think, *than in a place full of illusions?*

30

'This way, Flint,' I whisper.

We are taking a shortcut through Silas Kirby's farm.

It is all silent, and overgrown with hawkweed and brambles. The moon is rising above Silas's empty farmhouse. I wonder what would have happened to Grace if she'd stayed and married him? I look up at the dark windows, imagining my sister trapped inside. Just a ghost of herself now. Just a shadow.

Two huge tomcats are crouched in the farmyard, facing each other, staring each other out. One is tiger-striped, the other dirty-white with a missing ear. Flint's hooves clop across the yard, past the empty stables. The tomcats don't move. They don't even blink. I wonder how long they have been here like this

– locked in their silent battle. I wonder if they will stay here for ever.

We hurry on through the village, past our farm and out through the darkening fields, towards the main track across the marsh.

Towards the fayre.

The marshes open up on either side of us, great stretches of wetland yawning into the twilight.

The lane is empty.

A barn owl swoops across us – a fleeting sweep of silver and white – and then it has gone again. I shiver.

Was I right to come alone?

Yes. I couldn't have brought the others. I couldn't have put them in danger. I think of Grammy's words to me: *You'll find Grace. I know you will.*

'We need to be brave, Flint,' I say out loud. 'For Grace.'

Flint nods and prances importantly – a proud steed going into battle.

He seems steadier than the first time we set out together. Just as vain, just as clever and alert, but less flighty. He wasn't spooked by the barn owl. He has grown up a bit.

I wonder if I have too. I don't feel I have. I feel broken and lost and small and frightened.

Then Flint stops. He never just stops.

He is staring at the way ahead. He takes a step back. And another. He tosses his head and I can see the whites of his eyes, just as I did when we crossed Sorrow Marsh.

'Over here, Flint,' I whisper, nudging him gently towards the side of the track. The bulrushes are high on the other side of the narrow ditch. The ground looks solid enough there – sticky and cledgy, but not too wet. Flint moves quickly. He pauses at the ditch, waiting to be sure that I want him to cross it. 'Go on,' I murmur. Another encouraging nudge, and he leaps almost from a standstill, clearing the ditch by a mile and landing us safely in the reeds and rushes beyond. I climb down straight away. Flint looks at me and twitches his ears.

What are we doing?

'We're hiding, Flint,' I whisper, wrapping an arm around his head and stroking his velvety nose. 'We're hiding, and we're watching . . .'

In the story, the Marsh King is full of wicked tricks. I need to be clever if I am going to defeat him. I want to see him before he sees me . . .

The fayre is getting closer. I can feel it. My skin prickles.

I am worried the rushes aren't tall enough to hide Flint, but the fayre barely notices us as it passes by. People are talking, laughing. Animals doze in their rattling cages. A child spits cherry stones into the grass just inches from my feet.

My eyes search each cart, each caravan and carriage.

I am looking for the Marsh King. I am sure that he is here.

The final horse in the procession carries a lady with auburn hair. She is wearing a wine-red dress. Her heavy gold bracelets clink together and her necklaces gleam in the half-light. *The fortune teller*, I think. *The one who told Grace to run ...*

Her head turns as she passes by. She is the only person to see us hiding there in the reeds. She looks right at me, with her piercing black eyes. She shakes her head in warning, and mouths one word at me.

'*Go.*'

My heart cramps with fright. The fortune teller looks straight ahead again and keeps riding, following the procession of the fayre.

I crouch there, perfectly still for a moment, heart-beats jarring through me one after another. Then I stand up, mount Flint, leap back over the ditch on to the track, and canter to catch up with her.

She does not turn her head as we slow to a walk alongside her, Flint matching her chestnut mare stride for stride.

The fortune teller's hair glows like copper in the dying sunlight. 'Go away from here,' she says in a low voice, still looking straight ahead. 'You are not safe.'

I shake my head. 'You told my sister to run too. And she never came back.'

'Your sister?' She turns to look at me, then, as if she

has suddenly awoken.

'Aye, my sister Grace. You told her to run, to escape her fate.'

She stares. 'I remember her, I think. A girl with golden hair. Grace? That was her name?'

'That *is* her name,' I say. I won't talk about her as if she is dead.

'What happened to her?'

'She thought you meant to run from Hollow-in-the-Marsh, but you meant to run from *here*, didn't you? You meant for her to run from the fayre.'

The fortune teller looks at me, then her eyes flicker – panicked – as if she has seen something.

I turn quickly, but there is nothing there – only the darkening marshland. 'Is that what you meant?' I insist.

She nods. Her eyes are huge.

'He's here, isn't he? The Marsh King? He's hiding here, in the Full Moon Fayre?'

She says nothing. Her fingers tighten on the reins, her necklaces tremble on her chest.

I nudge Flint on, looking up at the carts and carriages ahead. 'I have to find Grace.'

'Wait.' The fortune teller reaches out and catches hold of my hand. She looks into my eyes for a second, then I watch in horror as her own eyes fill with tears.

I feel a swift dart of terror. 'What is it? You can see something in my future?'

'Something, yes . . . The mire, the lantern . . . Oh!'

A gust of wind rustles the bulrushes beside the road and their shadows dance across the fortune teller's face – bright and dark, bright and dark.

'Go home,' she urges. 'Go now!'

31

The triplets saw the fayre arriving in the village.

They know all about the bags of money Grammy has left them, and by the time I get home, Dolly and Deedee have theirs poured out on the kitchen table, stacking up the coins into little glittering towers.

'Put that away,' I snap, the second I step through the door. 'It's your inheritance. It's for important things. It's not for frittering away at the fayre.'

'But we want to buy new hats, Willa!' Dolly gushes. 'And a tiger!'

I blink.

'A pet tiger!' echoes Deedee.

Freya laughs, but I don't. They are making my head hurt. 'I don't think the tiger is for sale . . .'

'A puppy, then!' cries Dolly. 'We need a dog. Grammy kept saying we needed one, after old Bess died – to round up the sheep. And you said so too – don't you remember?'

'Fierce and loyal and black as a storm cloud,' Darcy says quietly. 'Like Thunder.'

'They don't sell puppies at the . . . It isn't that sort of fayre.'

But they aren't listening. 'And I want to go on *all* the rides,' Dolly interrupts, 'and see *all* the shows. And that monkey on a man's shoulder, and *everything*! Dadder wouldn't let us go last time—'

'Well, you're not going this time either,' I snap again. 'I said, *put that money away*!'

Fright flashes across their little faces and I hate myself. Tears start in my own eyes, hot and prickling.

'I'm sorry,' I mutter, sinking down at the kitchen table. I press my hands against my eyes. 'You can't go to the fayre. You just can't.' I am breathing hard, trying to stop the tears.

Freya is standing close to me. 'Don't,' she says in a low voice.

'Don't what?'

'Don't turn into Dadder.' And she goes upstairs, calling the triplets to come up to bed.

But Darcy doesn't follow the others.

'Where have you been, Willa?' she asks. 'Up on Glorious Hill, all that time?'

I open my mouth and close it again. I think of Darcy clutching the fire poker in her small hands; I think of that night she fell asleep with the fierce frown on her face – setting off to slay the Marsh King in her dreams . . .

'I just went for a ride,' I say. 'Flint needed to stretch his legs a bit.'

It is a lie, of course, and Darcy knows it, but she hugs me anyway.

She is still filthy from her day of digging Dadder's grave, so we put the tin bath by the fire and fill it up with water heated in pans. I wash her hair and comb all the tangles out.

'I'm sorry I snapped,' I say. 'They don't sell puppies at the Full Moon Fayre, though. Honest.'

She sighs. 'I didn't think they would.'

'Do you still talk to your imaginary pup? Thunder?'

She nods. 'Sometimes. When I'm sad.'

I try to smile. And she tries to smile back.

The fire crackles. We drink hot milk.

With each moment that passes, the night is growing darker, bringing me closer to the battle that must be fought. I am not going to hide from the Marsh King like the fortune teller said. I am going to hunt him down. I will wait until the fayre has set up on Silas Kirby's field, and then I will go there. Alone. I know it must be tonight, and I know there is a chance I will never come home again. Dark thoughts stalk through the silence.

Darcy is thinking too, but I don't know what about. She is very still. Her gold-brown eyes sparkle in the firelight. I weave her damp hair into a long thick plait. When at last we go to bed, she has bad dreams.

I hear her murmur, 'Here, Thunder. Come here, boy,' as she pats the blanket, calling her imaginary pup to snuggle up and comfort her. She hasn't done that for a long time now. It takes a lot to shake Darcy. She has buried her dadder today. Her grammy is gone. She has lost her biggest sister and now she is worried she is losing me too . . .

I lie awake. My mind is humming, humming like a swarm of bitey-flies. When I am sure everyone else is asleep, I creep into Grammy's room, taking Mammer's book with me – *Tales of the Marshes*.

I wrap Mammer's cloak around me and fasten it with her brooch, trying to feel close to her, trying to feel safe.

I scour the story of the Marsh King, searching for clues: *The marsh folk were afraid . . . that he would use his false flame to ensnare the souls of their loved ones . . . The evil sprite fed upon their fear – he grew fat and gleeful. He used folks' fears to control them, and the more frightened they were, the stronger he became . . .*

But how do you fight a magical being? How do you fight fear itself? It would be like fighting moonlight, or mist . . .

I wish it were a book of spells, like the villagers

imagine. There are no answers here. And I have no weapons. I have only myself, and I don't think I am enough. I am so tired. I am broken. I have always been broken.

I look out of the window. I can't see the fayre, but I can see the gauzy light of the fayre fires, amber in the blackness. And I think I can see a will-o'-the-wisp just beyond the fayre itself, floating pink and ghostly over Hollow Mire.

'I know you're there, Marsh King,' I whisper. 'And I know you've got my sister.'

I watch a moment longer. And I think perhaps he is watching me too.

We are like the two tomcats in Silas Kirby's yard.

'I'm comin' for you,' I whisper. 'Broken or not. I'm comin' for you.'

32

The summer night is all sweet with honey-suckle and dew-soaked grass, but there is an odd chill in the air. I pull Mammer's cloak around me. I tiptoe down the stairs and into the kitchen. I think I hear a noise, and I turn around, spooked, but all is quiet. I draw the curtains of Dadder's box bed; I feel strange enough creeping about like this, without thinking his ghoulish face is still in there peering out at me.

I go out to the stable, saddle up Flint and lead him across the yard. I close the gate as softly as I can. I think there is a flicker of movement above, and I look up to check I am not being watched from our bedroom window. But it is all still, all dark. Perhaps I was just hoping one of them would wake and come with me . . .

I climb up on to Flint and we set off together. I may have to leave my sisters behind, but being with Flint makes me feel braver.

I ride through the midnight village, and cut through Silas Kirby's deserted farm. The tomcats have gone, but there is a dark streak of blood on the cobbles; tufts of fur blow between brambles.

I wonder which cat won.

I grip the reins a little tighter and urge Flint on. We trot swiftly to the big field on the brink of Hollow Mire, then I tether Flint to the fence and walk towards the unfolding fayre – the dimly lit caravans, the opening awnings, the flaming braziers. I feel that juddering in my chest again. *Fate and fear, fear and fate . . .*

But before I reach the tents, a hand thumps on my shoulder. 'The fayre is not open for visitors, miss.'

I spin around, my heart thundering.

It is the showman. He is not dressed in his purple suit, and he does not have his tiger at his side, but I would recognize him anywhere. 'We are not open until tomorrow,' he says coldly.

He spins me around. 'Viktor, show this young lady off the site, please.'

Viktor appears from the shadows. When he sees me, he raises his eyebrows. 'You again?'

'Me again.'

'You know this person?' his father asks.

'She is looking for her sister,' Viktor answers. Then

quietly, to me: 'I told you – she's not here. Come on.' He takes my arm gently and walks me back towards the village, away from the fayre.

'You're wrong,' I whisper to Viktor, wriggling from his grasp as soon as we are out of earshot of his father. I stick my chin up. 'My sister *is* here.'

He stops. 'What makes you so sure?'

'She disappeared that night – when the fayre was here at Yuletide. Do you remember? You helped Freya look for us.'

'Yes. You and your other sister had been watching a show.'

'That's right – the shadow show. And then you said—'

'The what?'

'The *shadow* show. With all the shadow puppets. You know, that funny little tent right at the edge of the fayre. The man with the green eyes and the scarecrow hat . . .'

Viktor stares at me. 'There is no shadow-puppet show here at the Full Moon Fayre,' he says.

A weird icy feeling unfurls in my tum. The back of my neck prickles cold. 'No shadow show?'

'No. I am sure.' He looks anxious, confused. 'I don't think there has ever been a shadow-puppet show. You can ask my father, if you like?'

I turn and see the showman – still standing there with his arms folded, waiting for me to go. The giant is beside him now. And that conjuror – Albina. The three of them are side by side like a brick wall.

'No. Thank you, Viktor.' I don't need to ask his father.

Fragments of the Marsh King story are drifting and colliding in my head: *his cruel tricks, his dark magic . . . folk who were mere shadows of themselves . . .*

Mere shadows . . .

I swallow hard. At least now I know where to look.

I turn back, but the showman and the others are still standing there. They are all looking at me as if I am a trespasser – a scrumper, a poacher.

I glare at them, breathing hard, trying not to let them see the fear that is clutching at my insides.

They do not budge.

'Go on, scram!' an old woman calls out from just beside me. She is setting up her baked-apple stall. She flashes me a toothless grin. 'Go home! Come back tomorrow, my lovely, and bring all your little friends! Bring your gold and silver too!'

Flint and I plod back a little way towards the village, but I have no intention of going home. Not when I am so close.

When I check over my shoulder, Viktor has disappeared, and the showman and his cronies have gone back to setting up the big tent. I pull Flint around quickly and we trot to the near corner of the field, slipping down a bank of clay and leaping the ditch on to the squelching ground of Hollow Mire. I am holding my breath, checking that we have not been seen. The darkness is not enough of a cloak for Flint – he looks like a ghost horse in the gloom.

He doesn't like this ground underfoot, the sponginess of it. I can tell by the picky way he is placing his feet, finding a moonlit path through the darkness. But his surefootedness through the mire is why I need him with me now. We stay away from the filmy black water in the heart of the mire, skirting the edge of it, right around the outside of the fayre. The fayre folk are cooking their evening meals. They are talking, singing. There are shouts as the big tent is hauled up to standing.

We are here, just beyond it all. On the brink of reality, hiding quiet in the shadows. Toads creak in the shallow water at Flint's feet; eels slither in the oozing pools. I look out towards the middle of the mire – those great, dark stretches where no one in their right mind would ever set foot. I wonder if there are drowned faces there, hanging in the water, just like those I saw in Sorrow Mire.

Flint slips slightly in the sludge.

'Steady, Flint,' I murmur. 'Steady.'

At last we are there.

On the furthest corner of the field, I can see just one lonely, shabby little tent. We squelch towards it. The reeds are tall here, rustling and whispering as we pass.

I climb down from Flint's back, and crawl up a chalky scramble towards the higher turf of Kirby's field. I lie down against the chalk, peering over the top of the rise to check no one is around. 'Wait here, boy,' I whisper to Flint.

There is music coming from inside the tent. Half-sung, half-whispered: *The sky was black, the stars were bright, the waxen moon was gleamin'* . . .

I feel that juddering deep in my chest again, each heartbeat shaking me so hard I can barely breathe: *Grace! That's Grace's voice!*

I walk as softly as I can, even though I am sure the Marsh King knows I am coming. It feels like he is waiting for me. But there is no turning back now.

I stand for a moment at the entrance to the shabby tent. My sister's voice is clearer: *But still the damsel dreamt and dreamt, a-cursed to e'er be sleepin'.*

It is Grace – it is! She must be here, just inside . . . But when I push my way through the folds of white silk that cover the doorway, I find the little shadow theatre is dark and empty. It is so chilly I shiver. An old, round lantern hangs on a chain from the pitched roof of the tent – I remember it from when Grace and I saw the show back at Yuletide. There is a tiny light glowing within it – soft and pink.

Is it – could it be – the same lantern I saw bobbing like a ghost-light over Sorrow Mire?

Suddenly the hazy darkness is snuffed to pitch

black. I stop dead, unable to see my own hands in front of me. A draught snakes around my ankles, as if the doorway of the tent has breathed in and out, and I get a whiff of the mire – brackish, stagnant. I turn, but I can see nothing at all.

Then, as if it had indeed been waiting for me, the show begins. The tattered curtains are drawn back and the screen blushes with that weird pink light. I am shaking all over. I don't know what to do, so I watch . . .

A fire flickers high on a village green. The shadows of swifts and swallows glide and dive in the pink sky above. Music begins – a flute or a pipe – and a dancer appears. A shadow girl leaps and twirls about the fire, dancing wild as a whirlwind, blurred as a butterfly. But I know her the moment I see her. My heart lurches. *Grace!* Love and relief and terror flood through me all at once. She is here! But – what has she become? A shadow girl. A puppet in the shadowman's show.

I know what the Marsh King is doing: I can feel him plucking at my deepest fears as if they are the strings of a fiddle. He is taunting me. Using Grace to lure me in too, using my love of her to control me – and, oh! – the fear of losing her for ever.

'Grace!' I cry out – I can't help myself. I am sobbing now. '*Grace!*'

I run to the silk screen, scratching at it with my nails, taking great handfuls of it and ripping my way through. '*Grace!*' But she is not here. There is nothing behind the screen at all, just bare boards on the floor, the pale wall of the tent breathing in and out with the night breeze, and the oozing smell of the mire — stronger than ever.

There are shapes drifting around me — the shadow of my sister, the swifts and swallows — I can feel them cool as mist on my skin.

'Where is she?' I cry out. '*Where is my sister?*'

Then there is a movement in the furthest corner, beside the gathered curtain. I can just make out a dark, hunched figure.

It turns towards me.

33

Welcome. *You have been searching for me, I think, Willa Fernsby. Searching for something . . .*

The voice is everywhere at once. It is all around me – inside my head.

I squint into the darkness.

The hunched figure is just a silhouette against the pale wall of the tent. He raises his hands: they twitch and turn, and the shadows dance in the air. He is conducting them – an orchestra of stolen souls.

Then a quick, slashing movement. And the shadows vanish.

My heart is banging, I am shivering with sweat, but my voice is unwavering, defiant: 'Let me see you.'

Oh, you have seen me before.

The figure shifts slightly in the darkness – and I

think I see the outline of a scruffy scarecrow hat, grass-green eyes glinting in the gloom.

And you have been drawn to the light of my lantern. Do you remember?

Sorrow Marsh swims in my mind – the soft, pink light calling to me . . . Something is happening to me as the Marsh King talks: like sleepiness, like a spell. I try to drag myself from its grasp.

Trust me, Willa. Trust the light of my lantern . . .

There is a movement close to me – a spidery scuttling across the boards, the whiff of the mire.

Then a warm, pink flame flickers in the lantern. It bobs in the air – as if it is being carried on its chain. The light moves away from me, through the tent, disappearing out into the darkness.

I follow – I have no choice. As Grammy said, I have been looking for trouble all my life . . . *And now we know why.*

I touch Mammer's brooch – the triplets' magical omlet. I wish I had one of their wooden swords too, or Darcy's fire poker, or any sort of weapon at all. I swallow. I can see the pink light of the lantern, bobbing over the dark grass of the mire. I step out into the midsummer moonlight.

His whispering is all around me, and the lantern is a few yards ahead. So safe, so inviting . . . the glowing warmth of it. I can hear Grace's voice singing to me, beckoning me to follow: *A dreamin' and a dreamin' . . .*

That low whispering again, from the mire itself —
and inside my head: *You are so close now, Willa. You*
can join your sister here in the mire — oh! So peaceful. Rest
at last. I can see how tired you are, how frightened you have
been . . .

The lantern is calling to me.

Come to me, Willa Fernsby. We are old friends, you and I.
I know your deepest fears, the horrors that keep you awake at
night . . . Come home, now. Come and be a shadow like your
sister . . .

'My sister is not a shadow,' I breathe, trying to
claw back my thoughts from his grasp. 'We are not
shadows!'

I can feel his whispering all through me, magical
whispering, silvery as scissors. I can feel my body sinking down, my spirit drawn to the light of the lantern.
But I force my eyes to look around — to look down. I
am waist-deep in the mire now, and there are faces
floating around all me. Terror seizes me like the coils of
a great snake.

If I had a voice, I would scream for help, scream for
my grammy. A childish part of me still wants to believe
that, somehow, Grammy is the sundered soul who will
defeat the Marsh King at last . . . But no — Freya was
right. Sundered soul or not, Grammy is not coming
back. She said I would never be alone, but she was
wrong . . .

Hush now, Willa. Don't struggle. Just one more step . . .

I sink further into the mire — the icy darkness is chest-high now, slowing my breath, freezing my heart.

Oh, your soul, Willa Fernsby — your poor soul. I see it all now. Broken.

Broken — yes. I have always known it: I am broken inside.

Torn apart . . . Oh, there is suffering here. It will all be over soon. You are nearly here in my arms. Come and be a shadow, Willa — no more pain . . .

My heart is frozen. My mind is dull and numb.

Then I see something beside me — a flash of movement over the mire.

It is a boy. A dark-eyed boy. He is here, right next to me, moulded to that side of me where my soul is all ragged and broken and torn. His hand slips into mine as if it belongs there. He is holding me tight, holding me back.

Colt.

Tears are pouring down my face. My twin has found me. He has forgiven me. I have spent my life feeling torn in two, sundered from my twin, but he is here at last.

I gasp.

Sundered. Just like Gytha Greenwood.

I am a sundered soul . . .

34

Something changes in that moment. The whispering stops. I turn to see my twin's face, but he has gone. I can still feel the warmth of his hand in mine, though; I know that I always will. And there is something else in my hand now too: the old tinderbox.

My mind is turning once more, and my heart is no longer frozen. I feel stronger than I have ever felt before.

I drag my eyes from the light of the lantern, and I see the Marsh King's face for the first time. His skin is paper-thin, patched together with scraps. He is rotting away. He is a dying soul – a foul old fairy tale stuffed into a bag of skin. His grass-green eyes flash with fear, and the lantern trembles in the air.

Just one tiny step, he begs. *Just one!* The lantern

glows, desperately bright. *I can help you to be free of your fears. That terror that Grace may never come home; that horror that your mammer hated you! You can be free of it all — the sweet, sweet water of the mire will wash it all away . . .*

I want to tear the lantern from the shadowman's hand and smash it to pieces, but I don't. I can be brave without being angry. I won't be a fox in a henhouse any more. I can let go of all that now. I can be strong.

I see the frail figure before me, and the green eyes peeping out — the soul of a long-forgotten tyrant.

I see that this is no battle. The only weapon he has is fear. And fear can't hurt me if I won't be druv by it.

I know what I must do. I reach forward gently and open the little door of the lantern. The Marsh King watches helplessly as I pinch out the false flame with my fingertips. Then I take my tinderbox and stuff the last fragments of charcloth inside the lantern. I strike spark after spark. My breath is shallow and fast, the cold mire pressing at my chest. Its stink is in my throat, but my hands are steady now. At last, a spark catches on the charcloth, and it flares up into a bold yellow flame. A true light.

I take the lantern from his feeble hands.

No — please! the Marsh King moans. *Noooooo!*

There is a soft rushing sound. Voices all around, rustling together like marsh reeds; there is a stirring deep within the mire.

NOOOO.

With the snuffing of his false flame, the Marsh King is somehow crushed too. He sinks, limp and helpless. His spell is broken at last.

There is a soft splashing in the mire, a girl walking towards me, wading through the dark water. The light from the lantern is gold and bright as sun, and I can see her face as she gets closer. *Grace!*

She is pale as a ghost, thin and weak; her golden hair is wet and draggled. She is coughing, crying. I wade out towards my sister, wrapping my arms around her.

'Oh, Grace,' I sob. 'Oh, Grace!'

She clings to me. She can't speak. 'This way,' I say, pulling her back towards solid ground.

I see a movement out of the corner of my eye – a swooshing through the thick water. The Marsh King is behind Grace – closer, closer! He is reaching out for her with his filthy hands – trying to drag her back into the mire to die with him.

'No!' I scream, holding on to her tightly.

But then there is an almighty thundering of hooves and a *splash*, and something huge leaps through the air above our heads.

Flint!

He lands on the shadowman's chest, flattening him into the shallows of the mire. He prances and stamps while the Marsh King writhes beneath his hooves. The papery skin tears and darkness spills out of him, squirming like a thousand rats. And then there is a final, terrible sound – a bubbling scream – as the grass-green eyes close for ever, and the scarecrow hat sinks into the mud.

35

Grace and I try not to wake the others as we come into the house. I make a fire and cover her with blankets as she curls up in Grammy's old chair. I heat soup in the heavy-bottomed pan.

'Thank you,' Grace whispers. She eats the soup. She looks around the fire-lit kitchen as if she has just woken from a nightmare. She stares at the closed curtains of Dadder's box bed.

I tell her about Dadder, and Grammy, and that Silas Kirby has gone – disappeared into Sorrow Mire. I tell her about my journey to the edge of the Lost Marsh and back again, and how I found out about Colt, and all the other things that have happened while she has been gone. It takes a long time.

She listens, her lovely face pale and damp with tears.

'What happened, Grace?' I ask quietly. 'The night you disappeared?'

She breathes in and out. 'All I can remember is that I knew I had to leave. It was the only way to escape Silas Kirby . . .'

'You wanted to run away with the fayre?'

'Aye. And I remember standin' there at the edge of Kirby's field. They were all packing up the tents, gettin' ready to leave, and it was snowing . . . I remember somethin' calling me – so lovely – like a song of freedom. And then . . .'

'And then?'

'It was like I was stuck in a bad dream and I couldn't wake up. I remember feeling lost and calling out for Grammy, and wishing you were all with me. Sometimes it was sunset, and I was dancing. But mostly it was dark – so dark, and so cold . . .'

She is crying. I go to sit on the floor at her feet. I put my head on her knee.

She strokes my hair. 'And then there was a light,' she whispers, bending forward to kiss the top of my head.

At last the fire dies and we go upstairs to bed. But Grace doesn't turn towards our room, she goes into Grammy's room instead, and I follow. We sit down together on Grammy's bed.

'What is it?' I say.

'This.' And she gives me a piece of paper. It is crumpled and folded. A corner of it has been burnt.

'This is for you,' Grace says.

I smooth it out on my lap. And I know what it is straight away. It is the missing tale from Mammer's book: 'The Story that Never Was'.

This story isn't really a story at all. Nothing much happens. Just a lad growing up on a farm, running through the meadows with his sisters, lying in the sunshine, breathing and laughing.

'Oh! It's Colt,' I breathe, looking up at Grace. Tears are starting in my eyes. 'It's a story about Colt, isn't it?'

Grace nods.

I take a deep breath.

The boy's cheeks are red with running, the sunshine is in his eyes.

And perhaps he loves the horses and the sheep and the land, and he stays where he was born and grows up to be a farmer. Or perhaps he travels far and becomes a merchant or a mariner or a scholar. Perhaps he plays the pipe or the fiddle, and perhaps he doesn't.

There are no dramas in this story. He has no ogre to fight, no dragon to slay. At times he is pulled this way, or that way, but the lad is kind and strong. He knows himself and he knows what makes him happy in his heart. He anchors himself in the things he loves and the people who love him best. He finds his way through the marsh and the mire. And perhaps his life is a remarkable one, or perhaps it is very humble indeed, but it is truly the best life a person can hope to have. For he lives within his own skin as easily as an animal does.

He is wholly himself, and he is wholly happy.

I wipe the tears from my face with my sleeve.

'Dadder knew she'd written something about Colt, and he made me tear it out of the book. Told me to burn it,' Grace says. 'But I decided to keep it for you. Mammer would've told you, of course, but you were still so little when she died, and then Dadder . . .'

'I know,' I murmur. 'He couldn't bear to be reminded of what he'd lost.'

Grace nods again. 'He forbade us to speak of him – any of us.'

'Can you tell me . . .' I gasp and catch my breath, facing up to Dadder's cruel words at last, the deepest fear the Marsh King saw inside me. I try again. 'Did Mammer . . . Did she love me less because Colt died?'

Grace wraps her arms around me. 'No, no, no,' she murmurs into my hair. 'Mammer loved you so much, Willa. So much. And she would be so proud of you now.'

My breath goes in and out. I sob, and I let go of this terrible fear at last.

'It's why I could save you,' I whispered. 'Because Colt died. I'm broken, torn in half. Like Gytha Greenwood in the fairy tale – the sundered soul . . .'

Grace is smiling through her tears. 'I think you saved me because you are very strong, Willa, and very brave. And you believed that I *could* be saved.'

'I never stopped believing that.'

She looks at me, brushing another tear from my cheek. 'You're not half a soul just because you were born a twin, Willa.'

'Are you sure?' I whisper.

She almost laughs – and her smile is just as golden, just as wonderful as I remember. 'You are not half a soul. And you never have been. Is Darcy a third of a soul?'

And then I am laughing too, through my sobs. The idea is so ridiculous. 'No.'

'No, she is perfect and whole, and so are you. And you might once have been broken – I remember you as a baby. We couldn't comfort you, no matter what we did. But you were so tiny then, and it was so long ago – and look how strong you have become . . .' She smiles again. 'Have you still got that tinderbox?' she says.

I nod and reach into a pocket for it. It has not left my side since I ran away from home all those weeks ago. All the charcloth is used up now, but the flint still has good edges to it; the steel striker is still strong.

'This was Grammy's. She must have wanted you to have it when you set off looking for me.'

She takes the tinderbox from my palm. The old tin lid is worn and split, but it has been repaired – soldered with silver. Like a shining vein. Like a thread of starlight, or a lightning bolt.

'Grammy's mother was a silversmith,' Grace says. 'She made that brooch of Mammer's you're wearing.'

'The omlet?'

Grace laughs. 'Aye, the omlet. Well, Grammy's mother found this old tinderbox out near Hollow Mire, and she thought it was too lovely to throw away, so she fixed it – soldered it with silver, and gave it to her daughter.'

'It is beautiful,' I say, touching the smooth, gleaming crack. 'Broken but beautiful.'

Grace nods. 'More beautiful for having bin broken,' she says.

And she hugs me tight.

There are six of us back in our bedroom that night. Six beds side by side like cattle stalls. It won't be like this for ever, I know. The curse has no hold over us now. We are free.

'Do you still want to be a dancer, Grace?' I whisper from my bed.

'Aye,' she says, and I know she is smiling that dreamy smile. 'I would love that. One day. What about you?'

'I don't know yet. I love this farm, and the sheep and horses – more than I knew I did. I think I want to stay here. But it isn't because I have to: it's because I want to.'

'And does Freya still say she'll marry Fergus?'

'Aye.'

Freya grunts at the mention of her name and rolls over in her sleep.

'She will, and they'll have all sorts of adventures, I'm sure.'

'And the triplets will have their wild quests.'

We are quiet. Smiling.

'There *are* some places I'd love to go to,' I whisper. 'I want to go to the sea, and stand right in it with both my feet, and watch the waves and smell the fresh smell of it – not all marred by the muck of the marsh.'

'Aye – let's go to the sea!'

'We can go whenever we like. I have a map.'

'A map?'

'Aye. We won't lose our way. Not ever again.'

We lie there, staring and smiling into the darkness.

'I don't think I can sleep,' she whispers after a while.

'I can't either.' I feel like I will never sleep again. I wriggle beneath the bedclothes. 'It must be your turn for the scratchy blanket, Grace,' I say. 'You haven't had it for ages.'

She laughs. Then there is a different sound. Her breathing shudders a bit.

I get out of bed, and go to sit beside her. I hold her hand tightly.

'I never said goodbye to Grammy,' she whispers.

'I know.' I squeeze her hand. 'We'll go together, to Glorious Hill.'

I kiss her hair, and smooth it, and sit with her until she falls asleep at last.

I go back to my bed, but I am still wide awake. And I know Flint will be too, down in his stable – wide awake like a guard in the darkness, watching over us all.

36

I don't sleep a wink.

I watch the night deepen and fade. I hear owls and foxes. I hear my sisters snore and murmur in their sleep. And when the sun rises in the early hours of the morning, the darkness slinks away like a fox.

The others wake. We gawp at each other, and laugh. We clamber over each other's beds. We stare at each other over the kitchen table. The dawn sun shines in at the dusty windows – blinding bright.

'These are for you,' I say, and I give Grace her pile of books and her bag of gold from Grammy. 'She knew you would come home.'

We tell the others everything that has happened – Grace's story, my story: our very own fairy tale. 'The Sisters of the Lost Marsh', I will call it, and I will write it down in Mammer's book.

I will write down Grammy's story too: 'The Witch of Hollow-in-the-Marsh', because maybe Grammy was a witch after all, if 'witch' is the word for someone whose wisdom and strength are beyond the ken of normal folk – the word for a woman who won't be druv.

And I will copy Colt's story back into the book, where he will live for ever.

Two days later, when Grace is strong enough, we go together to Grammy's grave at the top of Glorious Hill.

She kneels by the elder sapling, saying words I can't quite hear. Her palms are flat on the warm ground; her tears fall into the summer grass; bees buzz in the clover.

There is a breeze today. Clouds are scudding across the bright sky, creating shadows that sweep over the hill and weave through the trees.

I look out over the marsh, towards the sea. Sunlight sparkles like daydreams on the dark puddles of Hollow Mire. It holds no more horrors for me now. The Marsh King has melted back into the pages of his fairy tale once more, and the mire is just a swathe of muddy marshland. I think about all the other souls who have lost their way out there – Amos and Sarah's father, and other men, women and animals too. I wonder if they saw the true light struck with Grammy's flint and steel. I wonder if some of them will be able to return home now, just as my sister did.

Grace is whispering some words over Dadder's grave now: 'To the earth, to the earth . . .' And then she is sitting down beside me, and linking her arm through mine. She puts her head on my shoulder and breathes in the sunshine. The air is all warm and musty with the heady scent of cow parsley. Cornflowers nod in the meadow like scraps of the sky. Dragonflies are zipping here and there – flashes of green, blue and gold beneath whirring wings.

'It's Midsummer's Eve, Grace,' I say. 'Shall we go to the dance tonight?'

'Aye,' she smiles. 'And we'll stay up to see the sun rise.'

Freya and the triplets are trooping up the hill towards us. Dolly and Deedee are waving wildly, and leaping and spinning and doing cartwheel after cartwheel, shrieking and collapsing into the tall, dry grass. There is a little shadow leaping about at Darcy's feet.

'Look 'ee, Willa! Grace, *look*!' Darcy calls. Her little face is beaming. 'He came to the farm this morning, just ran right into the kitchen like he lived there!'

They are close to us now. The shadow at Darcy's feet is not a shadow at all. It is a pup – a real little sheepdog pup. Black as a storm cloud.

'I'm goin' to call him Thunder!' Darcy says, her eyes shining. 'I can keep him, can't I? Please?'

Thunder? Thunder was Grammy's lost pup – the one who wandered out on to the mire more than fifty years ago. *It couldn't be, could it?*

'O' course you can keep him,' Grace smiles. 'So long as he doesn't belong to anyone else.'

Dolly shakes her head. 'He belongs to Darcy,' she says, quite certain.

And Deedee nods. 'Look – you can see he does.'

Darcy sits down next to us, lit up even brighter than the summer morning. The pup tramples in a circle, tail wagging. He nuzzles his nose into Darcy's warm leg and rolls over. She gazes and gazes at him: *he is real!* She strokes him, tickling his tum, pulling gently on his silky ears. She lies down beside him in the warm grass, burying her fingers in his soft black fur.

A girl and her long-lost pup.

He licks her hand. Darcy laughs and her long plait wiggles.

She is so like Grammy, I think . . .

All the pup knows is that this is *his* little girl, and she loves him. She has always loved him.

37

When we get home there are people in our farmyard. At first my heart tightens, remembering the dreadful night Grammy died. But today folk are here for a very different reason. They have heard that Grace is home. And it is the excuse so many of them have been waiting for – to make amends. They have brought gifts, peace offerings. Old Missus Cooper is here with all her gramsons – they've brought their scythes ready to start mowing our hayfield. Joss smiles shyly at Grace, tipping his straw hat to her.

The Mosses are here too. Fergus seems to have grown half a foot since I saw him last. He has brought six posies for us – buttercups and ragged robin, cornflowers and poppies. He blushes beetroot-red when

Freya kisses his cheek.

Missus Moss gives Grace a big, warm hug. 'You're home,' she says. 'Home at last, Grace. I'm so glad you're safe.'

'Darcy's got a new sheepdog pup!' Dolly announces loudly to everyone.

'He won't let us put a bonnet on him,' says Deedee sadly, 'but he's still nice.'

Mister Moss makes a fuss of Thunder and says he looks to be a very promising sheepdog indeed. Darcy beams proudly.

Old Missus Cooper is looking on. 'I'm sure we'll all miss the sight of you three pups scamperin' about the fields, though,' she says, and everyone laughs.

'It's a fine day for mowin',' someone says, looking up at the sky. 'Let's go to't!' The Cooper boys stretch and smile, and take up their scythes to start off for the hayfield. Fergus goes too.

Missus Cooper takes me to one side. 'I was wonderin', Willa . . .' She pulls a piece of paper out of her apron pocket; it is yellowed and coming apart at the creases. She checks that no one is looking. 'I got a *letter* once,' she whispers. 'I've kept it hidden forty years and more. Reckon'd it might a' bin from my sister, who left the marsh when I was just a babby. Travelled far away from here, she did, and we never saw her again. It come with a hawker one Yuletide. I thought it was – at least, I always *hoped* – it was from her. I was wonderin' if you might . . . help me.'

It is a weighty moment. And not just because Grammy's death is still so raw. It is a weighty moment for all of Hollow-in-the-Marsh.

It only takes me a second to decide, though.

'Aye,' I say. 'I will.'

I take the letter from her hand very carefully, scanning the faded ink. 'Was her name Bee?'

Missus Cooper's hand flies up to her heart. 'Oh!' she says in a hushed voice, her eyes filling with tears. 'Oh – yes! Beatrice! Bee! Does it say her name there? Can you show me?'

I point to the signature. 'Perhaps she wrote it thinking that you might learn to read one day.'

She laughs through her tears. 'Always was a wild one, our Bee.'

'Would you like me to read it to you?'

She takes the letter back, allows the old paper to fold itself, and tucks it back in her apron pocket. 'What I would really like, Willa, is to be able to read it myself. If you'd be so kind as to do a bit of teachin' to an old lady.'

I smile.

'Aye,' I say.

There is a lot of noise coming from the hay barn. The triplets are playing mountain climbers in there, scaling stacks of hay and then leaping off them from alarming heights. They are shrieking and laughing, and Thunder is yipping and running in little circles below them. But then, quite suddenly, it all goes quiet. The farmyard gate clangs shut. I turn around, and so do the other villagers.

It is Silas Kirby. He is standing right there – upright and alive and mean as ever.

'I've come for what's mine,' he growls.

The triplets have climbed down from their mountain. They are facing him, all in a row. Thunder is at Darcy's heels. I go quickly to stand beside them. Freya comes too, and then Grace. There is a muttering from the crowd behind us.

Silas smiles at Grace. An odd, dark smile. He bows. 'Grace Fernsby,' he says. 'My betrothed.'

Grace shakes her head. 'No, thank 'ee.' She is deathly pale, the same as when she waded out of Hollow Mire.

'None of us'll be marryin' you, Silas Kirby,' Freya says. 'We've got a farm to run. Plans of our own.'

His gaze travels over all six of us, and I see – I think I see – the flash of something horrible in his eyes. I have never noticed how green his eyes are – green as grass . . .

'So, that's how it is, is it?' he snarls. He goes over to the stable, and before anyone can stop him, he is wrestling Flint out into the yard. Flint drags his feet stubbornly, then he suddenly rears up, dashing at Silas with his hooves, catching him a sharp blow on the arm. The farmer curses. He raises his hand.

'*No!*' I say, stepping forward. 'Flint is ours now. He wants to stay here with us.'

Silas spits. 'I struck a deal with your dadder. And if I'm not gettin' my bride, you're not gettin' my horse. The elders agreed it was theft.'

Another mutter from the crowd.

'He's mine,' Silas goes on. 'An' I heard you've got my Silver too – stole her away and brought her back here, leavin' me stranded at Gallows End. Them's both mine. And I'm takin' 'em back.'

Flint dances away from him, twisting and bucking, then he prances across the yard, tossing his head defiantly.

Silas can't get near him. He spits in the straw. Then he storms into the stable and comes straight out again, pulling Silver by her grey forelock. 'I'll be back for that colt later,' he snarls. 'I'll bring my whip and teach him some manners.' He heads for the gate.

'Wait, Mister Kirby,' I call out. 'How much for both horses?'

'How much?' he growls. 'More than the pennies you chits 'a got in your pinny pockets, an' that's for sure.'

'Wait there,' I say. And I push past the crowd from the village and run into the house.

It only takes me a moment.

'Fair and square,' I say breathlessly, taking the small cloth bag and emptying all my gold into Silas's outstretched palm.

His eyes flash again – but it isn't anger this time. It's greed. 'This in't enough,' he bluffs. The corner of his mouth twitches.

'It's a fair price for these two horses,' I say.

'I'd say so!' says Missus Cooper, and people are nodding.

Silas Kirby's nephew Pete calls out: 'More 'an fair, if you ask me, Uncle Silas.'

'It's all you're getting,' I say. 'Take it or leave it. Either way, Flint and Silver are stayin' with us.'

'Take it or leave it,' Dolly pipes up. 'We won't be druv.'

'That's right,' echoes Deedee.

Freya nods. Grace folds her arms.

Silas puts his head on one side. His eyes gleam, grass-green. They do not blink. 'And what if I want more?' he says.

'We said, *WE WON'T BE DRUV!*' Darcy roars, and Silas staggers back. I have never heard my littlest sister raise her voice like that.

The noon sun glares in my eyes, and I rub them. *Were there . . . sparks?*

The crowd have moved forward. They are right behind us now – Mister and Missus Moss, Missus Cooper and all the others.

Silas Kirby has stopped still. He wants to laugh at Darcy, but he can't. He swallows his words. He backs away. I'd have backed away too. I'd have backed away if I'd been a wolf or a tiger or the giant from the Full Moon Fayre.

He pockets the gold, turns and walks away down the lane.

We watch him go.

Six sisters, side by side like a row of paper dolls.

Our Grammy is there with us.

And our Mammer too, and all the mothers before them.

They are in the earth beneath our feet, and the midsummer sunshine, and the soft breath of the marsh. They are in the bones of us.

Notes and Acknowledgements

The World, according to the
best geographers, is divided into
Europe, Asia, Africa, America,
and Romney Marsh.

Thomas Ingoldsby,
The Ingoldsby Legends

Sisters of the Lost Marsh is a rural gothic fairy tale inspired, in part, by the landscape of the Romney Marsh, Ingoldsby's 'Fifth Continent', which spans the counties of Kent and East Sussex in the south of England. Its salt-marsh meadows, reedy ditches, grazing sheep and lost villages were never far from my mind as I wrote the tale. The eerie, isolated beauty of Fairfield Church inspired the ruined fortress at Foulfield.

The seven mires of Willa's Lost Marsh do not exist, and indeed *mire* is a poetic indulgence rather than a geographical term. However, before the digging of the Royal Military Canal, before the formalized maintenance of drainage ditches, before the substantial sea defences, the Romney Marsh would indeed have been a considerably soggier, boggier place – much of it at the mercy of the tides: *The history of Romney Marsh is essentially the story of reclamation of land from the sea, the ongoing battle to drain it and to keep the sea from reclaiming it back* (theromneymarsh.net).

Many thanks to Owen Leyshon for his expert knowledge of marshlands, relayed via his brilliant sister, my editor, Rachel Leyshon.

I have borrowed some details from the history of this extraordinary place – the references to smuggling, for example, and the marsh fever too: the Romney Marsh was the last place in the UK to record cases of malaria – as late as 1910.

The aesthetic of this novel has been influenced by some wonderful art: John Piper's dreamy water-colours in his book *Romney Marsh* (1950); Annie Soudain's stunning contemporary prints of the marsh landscape; and sketches from *A Quiet Corner of England: Studies of Landscape and Architecture in Winchelsea, Rye and the Romney Marsh*, by Basil Champneys (1875).

The Lost Marsh dialect is a combination of authentic Kent and Sussex dialect (using, as reference, *A Dictionary of the Kentish Dialect*, Kent Archaeological Society, 2008) and some of my own inventions too. Grammy's instruction to the girls not to be *druv* – 'not by fear, not by nobody' – is inspired by the phrase 'We wunt be druv', a 'favourite maxim with Sussex people' according to the *Dictionary of the Sussex Dialect* (1875), quoted by Neville Hilditch in his compendium *In Praise of Sussex,* 1950. The phrase continues to be the unofficial motto of Sussex, featuring in poetry, on flags and indeed on bottles of beer from the Lewes-based Harvey's Brewery. 'We wunt be druv' is of course about strength, solidarity and stubbornness: the spirit of a free-thinking people.

Other sources of inspiration for the culture of Hollow-in-the-Marsh and the villages of the Lost Marsh include English folklore, and traditional and pagan celebrations such as Lammas, Beltane, Yule and the midsummer solstice. Thank you to my friend and fellow author Rebecca Smith for telling me about the 'witches' scratches' on her fireplace and the superstitions surrounding them.

Huge thanks to my beloved publisher Chicken House, and to all the fabulous Chickens: Rachel L, Barry, Elinor, Rachel H, Jazz (AKA linchpin), Esther, Sarah, Laura and Kesia. Rachel Leyshon, as always, is the person responsible for helping me to turn this big bag of ideas into an actual story – thank you, Rachel, for shining your true light when I felt well and truly lost in the mire!

Thanks to Helen Crawford-White for her breathtaking cover design, and for making all my books look just SO beautiful and perfect next to each other. Thanks to my fantastic copy-editor Daphne for helping me to whip this manuscript into shape.

Thank you to so many fellow authors and friends for your support and encouragement – the world of children's literature can be so lovely, and so generous.

Special thanks to all those who contributed kind words about this book, many of whom read it before it was even finished. Special thanks to Hilary McKay whose work I hold in such high esteem, and whose beautiful stories are so often my comfort and companion.

Thank you to my wonderful agent Luigi, to Alison, Hannah and all the team at LBA. Your time and support and enthusiasm for my work means so much to me. Thank you to Ellie at Speaking of Books, for bringing my stories and indeed my physical and/or online presence to schools and festivals all over the country.

Personal and heartfelt thanks to my gorgeous partner James, my little boy Fred, and to all the Stranges and the Barbers. I could not have written this book without your love and support (and your help with childcare too!).

Lastly, thanks to YOU for giving your time and your heart and your imagination to my story. Thanks to all the amazing people who keep the world of children's books turning: booksellers, publishing folk, librarians, reviewers, teachers, booklovers and Twitterers. I've said it before and I'll say it again: *Thank you for believing that good children's books can change the world, because they really can.*

Do follow me on Twitter @theLucyStrange for news, giveaways and updates on what's next . . .

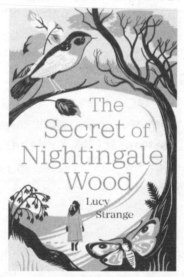

THE SECRET OF NIGHTINGALE WOOD

Something terrible has happened in the Abbott family and nobody is talking about it.

Mama is ill. Father has taken a job abroad. Nanny Jane is too busy looking after baby Piglet to pay any attention to Henrietta and the things she sees – or thinks she sees – in the shadows of their new home, Hope House.

All alone, with only stories for company, Henry discovers that Hope House is full of strange secrets: a forgotten attic, thick with cobwebs; ghostly figures glimpsed through dusty windows; mysterious firelight that flickers in the trees beyond the garden.

One night she ventures into the darkness of Nightingale Wood. What she finds there will change her whole world . . .

'Superbly balanced between readability and poetry [. . .] this is an assured debut.'
GUARDIAN

'Perfect in so many ways!'
EMMA CARROLL

Paperback, ISBN 978-1-910655-03-0, £6.99 • ebook, ISBN 978-1-910655-63-4, £6.99

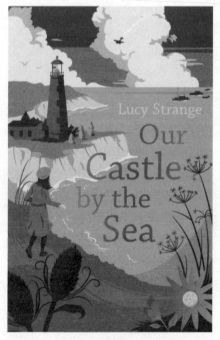

OUR CASTLE BY THE SEA

E ngland is at war. Growing up in a lighthouse, twelve-year-old Pet's world has been one of storms, secret tunnels and stories about sea monsters. But now the clifftops are a terrifying battleground, and her family is torn apart. This is the story of a girl who is small, afraid and unnoticed. A girl who freezes with fear at the enemy planes ripping through the skies overhead. A girl who is somehow destined to become part of the strange, ancient legend of the Daughters of Stone . . .

'A beautiful story.'
KIRAN MILLWOOD HARGRAVE

'This mesmerising novel is as much fairy tale as historical fiction.'
THE TELEGRAPH

Paperback, ISBN 978-1-911077-83-1, £6.99 • ebook, ISBN 978-1-911490-52-4, £6.99

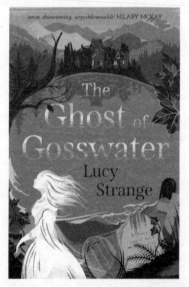

THE GHOST OF GOSSWATER

THE LAKE DISTRICT, 1899

The earl is dead and cruel Cousin Clarence has inherited everything. Twelve-year-old Lady Agatha Asquith is cast out of Gosswater Hall to live in a tiny, tumbledown cottage with a stranger who claims to be her father. Aggie is determined to discover her real identity, but she is not alone on her quest for the truth. On the last day of the year, when the clock strikes midnight, a mysterious girl of light creeps through the crack in time; she will not rest until the dark, terrible secrets of the past have been revealed . . .

'One of those eerie, shimmering, unputdownable books . . .'
HILARY MCKAY

'Creepy, funny, moving, empowering . . . this stayed with me long after I had finished it.'
NATASHA FARRANT

Paperback, ISBN 978-1-911077-84-8, £6.99 • ebook, ISBN 978-1-913322-61-8, £6.99

THE ISLAND AT THE END OF EVERYTHING
by KIRAN MILLWOOD HARGRAVE

Ami lives with her sick mother on an island where the sea is as blue as the sky. But the arrival of a cruel government official changes everything. Her island is to become a colony where only sufferers of leprosy may live.

Taken from her mother, Ami is sent to an orphanage across the water. Here, she meets a honey-eyed girl called Mariposa, and together they make a daring plan to escape back home to the world she loves.

'. . . such a fiercely kind and generous book, and so finely-wrought and so full of light . . . brilliant.'
KATHERINE RUNDELL

'A passionate but delicately told narrative of great courage and kindness . . . a gripping adventure from which many lessons can be drawn.'
THE GUARDIAN

Paperback, ISBN 978-1-910002-76-6, £7.99 • ebook, ISBN 978-1-911077-47-3, £7.99

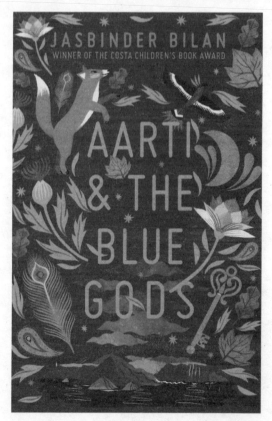

AARTI & THE BLUE GODS by JASBINDER BILAN

Aarti has lived nearly her whole life on the island. Orphaned as a little girl, she has been taken care of by Aunt, whose temper is as stormy as the weather.

Aarti's only comforts are her pet fox, Chand, and a colourful storybook about the Hindu gods. Then one day, she finds a tatty toy rabbit hidden in a locked room and memories of another time and place start to surface. She begins to suspect Aunt has not been truthful about who she and Aarti really are . . .

Paperback, ISBN 978-1-913322-59-5, £7.99 • ebook, ISBN 978-1-913696-29-0, £7.99